SECRETS BEHIND
THE HEDGES

SECRETS BEHIND THE HEDGES

SAMANTHA DUPREE

Secrets Behind the Hedges

Samantha Dupree

FIRST EDITION

ISBN: 978-1-7355039-2-9 (hardcover)
ISBN: 978-1-7355039-0-5 (paperback)
ISBN: 978-1-7355039-1-2 (ebook)

Library of Congress Control Number: 2020914384

MH
Morrison House

Contents

May you go
from strength to
strength

Prologue

Olivia Elizabeth Whittaker Donovan, known by everyone as simply "Liv," lowered her paint brush and stepped back to get a better view of the wall. She smiled. The scene was coming along nicely. When finished, the whole wall would look like an enchanted forest. With the brush, she was creating tree trunks and branches. The branches ran progressively narrower as they flowed outward from the trunks, intertwining into a fine mesh that formed a canopy of leaves that Liv's husband was creating using small sponges dipped in varying colors of green paint. The room was a basement on its way to becoming a playroom for the couple's two boys—William, age six, and Jeffrey, age three.

"Looking good!" Liv grinned. Curvaceous yet toned, with platinum blond hair and crystal blue eyes, Liv enjoyed being a mom. A schoolteacher by trade, she'd taken off to be a stay-at-home mother for at least a few years. She'd go back to teaching eventually, but for now, she was more than content to take care of her boys. And in the basement on that afternoon, working with her husband, with the snow falling outside and piling up in the window wells, there was no place else she'd rather be.

"Well, it better be," Kurt replied. Kurt Donovan, tall and chiseled with close-cropped, coffee-brown hair framing a square face, was taking a rare weekend off to help Liv with the basement project. When they'd purchased the home in Arlington, twenty minutes from Kurt's work at the Pentagon, he'd promised to spend more time with Liv and the kids, but it hadn't worked out that way. The hours were long and weekends seemed to be hit or miss, with Kurt working most of them. Liv understood; at least she understood the demands. As to what exactly Kurt did, Liv had only a vague idea.

"What's that supposed to mean?" said Liv.

"Well, it just means that I'd hate to think I spent a perfectly good Saturday working on something like this for no reason."

"Well, it's going to be beautiful. Just wait until it's done. The kids are going to love it." Liv had watched as her husband had progressed through the ranks of the US Navy, starting as a cadet at Annapolis, spending time as a Navy SEAL, and then landing the position at the Pentagon in intelligence, working as some kind of liaison with intelligence counterparts in Europe. Kurt never volunteered too much information about his day-to-day responsibilities and Liv never asked, knowing Kurt's top-secret clearance would have precluded him from saying very much anyway.

"You know, Liv, we could have hired somebody to do this. It's not like the old days. We have some money now. We can afford it."

"Oh sure, but we want to do it ourselves, don't we? I mean, it's a playroom for *our* kids. Besides, aren't you having fun? I am."

"Fun with these little sponges? Oh, sure, it's a blast. Maybe we can do the whole house like this."

"Oh, c'mon. *I* think it's fun. Besides, we get to do something together, just the two of us. We get to create something magical for our children."

"I guess so. I'm just saying that if we wanted to, we could bring in a professional artist and really do it right. For too long, we've had to cut corners. I don't want to do that anymore, Liv. You know where I've come from. All my life, I've sworn that I'd eventually be in a position where I can live the way I want to live. Where *we* can live the way we want to live."

"Well, sure, and here we are. We made it. But that doesn't mean we can't still do some fun do-it-yourself projects from time to time."

"Wait—you mean you think we've made it?" Kurt asked, furrowing his brow.

"Sure."

"You're happy with where we are?"

"Of course. Aren't you?"

"You don't want more?"

"More what?"

"More…everything!"

"I have my wonderful husband, my two adorable kids, and the perfect house. What else is there?"

Kurt was silent for a long moment and then finally said, "Liv, let me ask you this. Let's stipulate that where we are right now is fine. We're in a good place. Okay. But what about the future? Imagine yourself at fifty. What does your life look like? What do you have? What do you want?"

Liv looked off into space for a second or two and then replied, "Our boys have grown into fine men who are terrific husbands and fathers, I've made a difference in the lives of my students, you and I are enjoying a wonderful relationship that's only gotten stronger over the years, and I'm still as happy as I am right now."

Kurt nodded slowly, but Liv sensed just a trace of something in his eyes. Was it cynicism? Disappointment?

"What about you?" she said, warily. "Where do you see your life at fifty?"

"Well, listen, Liv, everything you just said is nice, but…"

"But what?"

"But, well, I have our sights set a little higher, that's all. Don't get me wrong. What we've got is a good start. But I've got some goals."

"What kind of goals?"

"By the time I turn fifty, I'm going to be wealthy, Liv. I mean really wealthy. Not just rich. Oh, no, rich won't do it. I'm talking *wealth*. I'm glad you like this house, but we're going to be living in one five times this size. A mansion somewhere on the water. We'll have a boat. A *big* boat. I'll have a Ferrari. You'll have all the jewelry you could ever want. Our regular checking account will have a balance that will never dip below a cool million dollars. You want to go to New York for dinner? We'll hop aboard our private jet."

"A mansion? Ferrari? A private jet?" Liv looked slightly alarmed.

"You bet. And we'll take trips around the world. We'll get William and Jeffrey into the best schools money can buy. Stick with me, babe. I'm taking us places."

Liv became quiet and turned towards the wall, taking her brush and pretending to add some detail to the painting, flicking the bristles over an already-painted branch. It wasn't as if she didn't appreciate Kurt's aspirations. He always had a lot of energy and drive; it's one of the things that attracted her to him in the first place. But there was something about this sudden revelation that wasn't sitting quite right.

Quietly, she finally said, "Kurt, I didn't know you wanted all that. Are you not happy with what we've got right now?"

Kurt hesitated a second and then said, "Happy? Oh, well, sure. Of course. I mean, sure. Look, don't get me wrong, Liv. It's just that our lives can be so much better. Don't you want more things? A bigger house? Jewelry? Trips?"

"Not really. I mean, I guess I never really thought about it. I'm just happy where we are. I always figured the future would take of itself."

"Well, I'm not going to apologize for my ambition," Kurt said impatiently. "Really, Liv, I don't get you. Who doesn't want more? You should never be happy with what you have. You should always be striving to do better. That's what it's all about." Then, sensing he was pushing his limits with his wife, he forced a grin and cheerily added, "You'll see. I'm going to give you the world!"

Liv smiled meekly in return. Then Kurt Donovan continued to dab his sponge onto the branches she had finished, not noticing that his wife's eyes now glistened slightly as she turned from him and dipped her brush back into her can of paint.

CHAPTER 1

FAMILY TRADITIONS

I t was not as if Liv was unaccustomed to money. Coming from the family she came from, she was, in fact, much more accustomed to it than Kurt. Perhaps that explained Kurt's ambition. He came from nothing. *Maybe he was overcompensating*, Liv would think to herself whenever she would replay the basement conversation in her head. There was having money, and there was flaunting it.

Liv came from old money. Her family's business, Gallagher Construction, was started in 1850. Liv's great-great grandfather came to America from Ireland due to the potato famine. He settled in Summit, New Jersey, where he built homes in the area, eventually expanding his operations along the New Jersey shoreline from Asbury Park to Lavellette. Liv's grandfather William eventually became the president of the company. All of Liv's uncles, cousins, and even her father worked there. She was proud of the family business and how hard everyone had worked to keep it running for generations.

As a child, Liv was taught the importance of family. Her family sat down and had dinner together every night. Her weekends and summers were spent in Bay Head at the family beach house that her great-grandfather built. Her grandmother, whom Liv was named after, was the nurturing grandmother, dispensing love and wisdom to all of her grandchildren. "Family first" was more or less her mantra. Holidays were extra special for the family with Liv's grandmother seeing to every detail, whether it was Christmas, Easter, or Halloween in Summit, or the Fourth of July in Bay Head. For Thanksgiving, Liv's grandparents sprung for an annual trip for the entire family to Florida, putting everybody up at the exclusive Breakers Hotel in Palm Beach. It started out intended as a one-time thing, but it became a cherished family tradition. For Liv's grandmother, no matter the holiday, it was always about remembering the people in your life and expressing your affection for them.

And so none of Liv's childhood was about the money, really. She was surrounded by it, but it wasn't anything that was ever emphasized. In fact, although the construction company did quite well when she was growing up, Liv and her family lived modestly. Her father, like everyone in the company, had to start at the bottom and work his way up. There was never any favoritism or nepotism. Because of this, Liv understood the value of hard work. Her parents' house was a humble house built by, and rented from, the company. Starting at the age of twelve, it was expected that Liv take a summer job. Once in high school, she also had to get an after-school job.

Liv's father, Peter Whittaker, was right at home with the Gallagher work ethic. He never took a thing for granted, especially including his position with Gallagher Construction. Still, as hard as he worked, normal construction hours allowed for him to be home every afternoon. He was long gone in the mornings by the time Liv and her younger sister, Sarah, got up, but he was always back to greet them when they returned home from school. Family time was treasured more than any paycheck. Liv's mother, Victoria, was a wonderful cook, a talent she shared with both her daughters. Liv would always recall with great fondness the evening dinners—the warm meals and the lighthearted banter around the table.

In her teens, Liv often dreamed about the kind of man she would one day marry. It would be a man very much like William. In addition to being a hard worker and good provider, her father was a capable man. The house and lawn were always in good shape. So was the family car which her father prided himself on keeping in top condition, insisting on doing all of the routine maintenance himself, and even most of the major mechanical work. He made improvements to the house often, building a deck one year that he enlisted Liv to help with, to teach his eldest daughter how to build something that she could take pride in. One summer at the shore, he and Liv and Sarah built purple martin bird houses. The girls' father was attentive in other ways, too. Every Valentine's Day, he brought home a dozen roses each for his wife and two daughters. Maybe it was just a fantasy, Liv often thought, to believe she would one day meet a man as good as her father, but it was a fantasy she felt was worth pursuing. Why settle for anything less?

Liv knew from a very young age that she would one day pass along the values learned in childhood to her own family, providing them with the same stable and loving environment that she grew up in. To her, family was all that mattered. Did Kurt understand that? Maybe they really were from two different worlds. Liv sometimes wondered if she made the right choice by marrying him. She often thought back to her college days.

CHAPTER 2

STRANGERS IN THE NIGHT

It was Liv's second day on campus. While making trips back and forth from her roommate's car to their new dorm room across the quad, Liv heard music and singing. When she looked up, she saw a handsome young man on the second-story balcony, singing along with a boombox to the sounds of Frank Sinatra's "Strangers in the Night." The young man saw Liv take notice and he pointed at her. Then he picked up his boombox and slowly descended the stairwell, all the while continuing to sing to her. When he finally reached her, he dropped to one knee and asked her if she would please have dinner with him. Liv didn't know whether to be flattered, embarrassed, or petrified.

"If you say no, I'm just going to continue to sing to you," the young man said. He was probably six-foot-one, thin but muscular, with jet black hair, blue-green eyes, and a captivating smile.

"Okay, okay," Liv replied, and they agreed to meet the next evening in front of Liv's dorm room. The young man's name, Liv would learn, was Ryan Murphy. And the next night, apologizing for not having any mode of transportation, he walked Liv to the

4

nearest eating establishment, a Taco Bell. Over tacos and fajitas, Ryan told Liv all about himself. He was from Naples, Florida, and was in the ROTC program at school as a US Marine. He was a drama major, and worked part-time at the front desk of one of the local hotels. He came from a close family. He had two brothers and two sisters. His mother was a high school teacher at a Catholic school, and his father was an accountant. Liv noticed the cross around Ryan's neck and asked him about it. It was from his first communion, he told her. His faith was very important to him.

Somewhere during the evening, Liv realized that she couldn't stop smiling. She hadn't known him long, but she liked Ryan. She was certain of it. The two walked around campus after dinner, and then Ryan eventually walked Liv back to her dorm room. He leaned forward and kissed her. "I've been wanting to do that all evening," he smiled. Then he added, "Listen. I know Taco Bell isn't exactly five stars, but maybe you could let me come over and cook dinner for you tomorrow night."

"Well, you're welcome to try," said Liv, "but I only have a microwave in my dorm room."

"Ah, but I can work magic with a microwave. You'll see!"

The next evening, Ryan came as promised. He laid a blanket on the floor, lit some candles, and set out some paper plates and plastic silverware. Then he pulled out two plastic wine glasses and two bottles of Chianti. And, of course, he brought his boombox to play more Sinatra.

Much to Liv's surprise, with nothing but a microwave, Ryan managed to make a wonderful dinner. Tossed salad, spaghetti, and garlic bread. Liv loved how thoughtful and romantic Ryan was. After dinner, he asked her to dance, and he sang softly in her ear. The night ended with Ryan spending the night.

Liv liked to tell her friends and family that Ryan came for dinner and never left. They dated for the next two years. It was a comfortable relationship. Stable, even predictable. The two took an apartment off campus. They played tennis after class, took their beagle Buddy for long walks, and cooked dinner together every night. Friday night was always date night.

The second summer they were together, Liv was visiting Ryan's family in Naples. She'd become close to them. One evening during the visit, Ryan took her to the mall. They walked past Bailey Banks & Biddle jewelers, and he asked her to go in. Then he asked the woman behind the counter if they could look at some engagement rings. Liv wasn't completely surprised. The couple had been talking about getting married for some time. It was the next logical step, after all. Liv smiled as she tried on the different rings, finally finding the one she loved. "We'll take it," Ryan declared. And, just like that, Liv and Ryan were engaged.

The wedding would be held in Florida two days after graduation. Liv was settled and happy. She was going to marry her best friend. But yet, perhaps, there was a piece of her that yearned for a little more excitement.

CHAPTER 3

SUMMER LOVES

It was the summer of Liv's junior year, summer at the Jersey shore. What could be better? She was excited about being home and loved spending time with her family and catching up with her summer childhood friends. And that year, she decided to volunteer on the labor and delivery floor of nearby Point Pleasant Hospital. She loved babies. Plus, she knew the experience would look good on her teaching résumé.

She missed Ryan, of course, but he was off on an ROTC tour that summer in Quantico. Liv had taken Buddy to the shore with her. Liv and Ryan wouldn't see much of each other, but they both looked forward to Memorial Day. Ryan would have the weekend off, and Liv had invited him to the annual Memorial Day block party at her family's shore house, a summertime tradition that Liv absolutely loved.

When Memorial Day arrived, the block party started out like it did every year. A long buffet table was set up on the beach and all the families on the block brought two dishes each. Everybody brought blankets, lawn chairs, and, of course, alcoholic beverages. There was a bonfire and fireworks scheduled for the evening. Liv was introducing Ryan to her neighbors when, out of the corner of her eye, she saw a tanned man with gorgeous brown curly hair wearing a pink polo shirt and white linen pants. It was David Santoro, and she was surprised to see him. David was four years older than Liv. His grandparents owned the house across the street and their families had known each other for over sixty years. Liv and David had been great childhood friends, but she hadn't seen him in a couple of years. He'd graduated from the University of Miami and had started his own successful flower import company in Miami.

Liv was excited to catch up with him. In the buffet line, she hugged him and introduced him to Ryan. "I hear you two are getting married," David said. "Ryan, you better always treat her right. We're like family, you know."

David explained that he'd come back home for the summer to help out his grandmother. She'd been overwhelmed after his grandfather had passed away not long before, and he arranged to run his business out of her house for the summer.

As they talked, David suddenly began to see Liv in a completely different way than he had when they were kids. She was no longer the little girl across the street. She had grown into a beautiful, mature, confident, and sexy woman. His family had always adored her, especially his grandmother and mother. Growing up, they used to tease him and say, "One day you're going to marry that Olivia Whittaker!" David would always laugh. But he suddenly didn't find the idea so silly.

At the end of the weekend, Liv walked Ryan to his car and they said their goodbyes. She knew she wouldn't see him until they'd return to school at the end of August, and she would definitely miss her best friend.

The summer progressed, and as it did so, Liv found herself spending more and more time with David. They enjoyed the same things—swims in the ocean, long walks on the beach looking for shells and sea glass, Sunday family barbecues, and miniature golf. They went to the boardwalk together and to an occasional dinner. She loved spending time with him and she enjoyed getting to know the man she had grown up with.

One night, Liv and her mom were enjoying a glass of wine on their deck, watching the full moon beginning to ascend in the sky. David came strolling up the boardwalk towards the deck. "Liv," he said, "would you like to go down to the lifeguard stand to watch the moonrise?" Liv smiled and nodded. Watching them as they walked over the dune, Olivia's mom couldn't help but smile, too. She liked Ryan Murphy, but she felt that David Santoro was a much better match for her daughter.

Down at the lifeguard stand, David helped Liv up onto the tall seat, then sat down beside her. They looked up at the moon, its light reflected off the gentle ocean waves. David placed his hand on top of Liv's. Then he began spinning the engagement ring on her finger. "Liv, I really need to tell you something," he said. "I think you're making a huge mistake."

"What do you mean?"

"I don't think you should marry Ryan. I believe that *we* are meant to spend the rest of our lives together, Liv. Here, on this beach, watching our children play just as we did, and our parents, and their parents. We belong together."

Liv looked deeply into David's charming hazel eyes as he leaned in and kissed her under the moonlight. In her heart, she could easily imagine a life with David. A beautiful life.

That night she lay in her childhood bedroom and stared at the ceiling. She had a big decision to make and she prayed it would be the right one.

CHAPTER 4

CHEERS TO ROMANTIC MORNINGS, EVENINGS, AND AFTERNOONS

The next day was Sunday, and on Sunday mornings, Ryan always called. Like clockwork. Sure enough, 9:00 a.m. on the nose, Liv's phone rang.

"Hi, Ryan," she answered. "How are you?"

"Well, you know. Same old same old. PT drills and a lot of basic training. I have good news, though. I found out that I'm getting the Fourth of July weekend off, so I can come back up there to see you. Isn't that great?"

Liv's hand started to sweat as she held the receiver. She swallowed hard.

"Liv?" said Ryan. "Did you hear me? Are you there?"

"Yes, yes, I'm here, Ryan. Listen, do you remember meeting David Santoro over Memorial Day weekend?"

"David Santoro? Sure. Great guy. Super friendly."

"Well, you know I told you that David and I have been spending time together."

"Sure."

"Well, last night, he asked me to go down to the beach to watch the full moon rise."

"Just like you, Liv! You've always been obsessed with full moons."

"Yes, well, anyway, something happened on the beach."

"Something happened? Like what?"

"Well, listen, Ryan, this isn't easy for me to say, but, well, David kissed me."

"Liv—what? What did you just say?"

"David kissed me."

There was a long pause before Ryan answered. "I'll kill him," he said at last.

"Hold on, Ryan."

"Liv, did you kiss him back? Do you have feelings for him? Liv, what the hell's going on?"

Liv felt the room spinning. She took a deep breath, trying to compose her thoughts. "Yes, Ryan. I'm sorry. Yes, I have feelings for David. Spending time with him has made me realize something. You and I—we're missing something in our relationship. Something big. We're missing *passion*, Ryan. The kind of passion that gives you butterflies, that makes your heart sing, that makes you want to spend every second with someone. Ryan, I love you. I really do. I probably always will. But I know in my heart that marrying you would be the wrong thing. For both of us."

There was nothing but silence on the other end.

"Ryan? Are you there? I'm sorry to have to tell you this, Ryan. I really am. Please say something. Ryan?"

Then all Liv heard was a dial tone. The engagement was over.

Liv knew she'd miss her best friend. But there was also no mistaking that her heart now belonged to David. The following day, she sent her engagement ring back to Ryan, overnighting it so that her decision would be made clear.

As the summer wore on, Liv fell more and more in love with David. There were moonlit walks on the beach, romantic dinners, and lovemaking in the ocean at dawn. Liv couldn't get enough of David and David couldn't get enough of Liv. This was the love that Liv had been dreaming of her entire life.

August came much too quickly for them both. Soon, enough, Liv would have to return to school and David would need to get back to his business in Miami. One afternoon towards the end of the summer, Liv came home from her job at the hospital and David was waiting for her in the driveway. "Liv, guess what? I got us into that new restaurant in Brielle, on the bay, the one we've been dying to try."

"Really?" Liv smiled. All summer, she'd wanted to go to the new Brielle River House restaurant.

"I'll come back over at seven to pick you up," David said, then he kissed her and ran back across the street. Liv dashed upstairs and told her mother, then went into her bedroom and tried on a dozen dresses, finally settling on a stunning white dress with gold embroidery that she'd been saving for a special occasion. At exactly seven, David was at her front door, looking incredible in a Brooks Brothers navy blazer, a crisp white shirt, khaki slacks, and beautiful Ferragamo loafers.

The restaurant was even nicer than Liv had imagined. There were candles everywhere and on every table there were white and blue hydrangeas. A man was softly playing a piano in the corner. The host led David and Liv to a table that overlooked the bay. It felt like a dream to Liv.

"We'll have a bottle of Opus One," David told the waiter.

"Wow," said Liv.

"Tonight is about celebrating our love for each other," David said, taking Liv's hand. Then he leaned across the table and kissed her.

The dinner was perfect. From the wine to the food to the romantic atmosphere. Liv didn't want the evening to end.

When they returned to her home, David walked her to the front door. There, Liv noticed a path of candles leading from the boardwalk to the deck.

"What's all this?" she said.

"Just a little something I put together," said David. "With the help of your mom."

Together, they followed the candles and walked up onto the deck which was covered with red rose pedals. There was a bucket with a bottle of Dom Perignon champagne and two champagne flutes. Music was playing from the speakers softly. Fred Astaire was singing "The Way You Look Tonight."

David opened the champagne and poured the glasses, handing one to Liv. "Cheers to romantic mornings, evenings, and afternoons," he said. "And to a lifetime of happiness." He touched his glass to hers and they sipped the champagne and then David said, "Liv, may I please have this dance?"

They danced slowly on the deck under the star-filled sky. When the song ended, David dropped to one knee, and out of his pocket he pulled a Cartier ring box. He opened it, and said, "Olivia Elizabeth Whittaker, will you make me the happiest man alive and please be my wife?"

The ring was the most gorgeous ring Liv had ever seen. She could barely breathe. "Yes, David! Yes! Of course!"

David stood and placed the ring on Liv's finger and kissed her. "We're going to have a lifetime of happiness," he said. "Now, if it's okay with you, I'd like to make love to my fiancée."

David grabbed the bottle of champagne and a couple of beach towels and then took Liv's hand, leading her down to the beach. "I want to make love to you under the stars," he said, laying out the towels. They sat beside each other and kissed passionately. Then Liv rose to her feet, facing David. She slipped off her dress. It fell to the sand and she stood in front of him now completely naked, never having felt more desirable or more like a woman.

"Liv," David breathed. "My God…you're so beautiful."

Liv placed one leg on each side of David and then knelt down, straddling his body. She leaned forward and kissed him as he reached up and cupped her breasts in his hands, slowly kissing them. A moment later, Liv felt David inside of her. She loved the way he felt. "We're going to make beautiful babies," he whispered in her ear.

They made love for hours. Afterwards, they lay in each other's arms, naked, staring up at the stars with the sound of the gentle surf in the background. Could life get any better?

CHAPTER 5

THE INN AT LITTLE WASHINGTON

At the end of August, Liv headed back to Roanoke in her Honda Accord with Buddy the beagle in the passenger seat and a five-carat diamond ring on her finger. *What an incredible summer*, she thought to herself.

It was her senior year and she'd decided to keep the apartment that Ryan and she had been sharing. Ryan had returned to school the week before and had moved out. It was strange for Liv to be back in the apartment without him, but she knew she'd made the right decision. With all her heart and soul, she loved David. She was also excited to start her new teaching internship at Crystal Springs Elementary School where she was scheduled to have twenty-four students in her kindergarten class. Everything in her life seemed to be falling into place.

For Labor Day weekend, Liv planned to get her classroom set up. The first day of school would be the following Tuesday. But arriving back to her apartment that Friday, she knew immediately that her plans would have to wait. Standing in front of her door, looking as handsome as ever, was David.

"David! What on earth are you doing here?!" she said.

"I decided I couldn't let my fiancée spend this long weekend alone," David smiled. "I have a surprise for you. We're spending the weekend at a five-star hotel. The Inn at Little Washington."

Liv was speechless.

"I need you to hurry up and pack," David continued, "because we need to get on the road!"

Liv, who was notorious for overpacking, ran upstairs and began packing a pair of suitcases as fast as she could. Then she made arrangements for her neighbor to take care of Buddy and she and David were soon on the road. The drive through the Blue Ridge Mountains was stunning, and in seemingly no time, they arrived at the Inn, a charming two-story grand home.

David and Liv checked in at the front desk and the bellman took them to their room. They passed through the opulent dining room, complete with red velvet covered chairs and couches and gold light fixtures. Then they passed through a romantic courtyard with a rose garden and a beautiful fountain. When they made it to their suite, Liv took it all in—the old, four-poster bed in the center of the room, the woodburning fireplace, the antique claw-footed tub in the bathroom. Everything oozed romance.

Liv began to unpack but realized to her dismay that she'd forgotten her cocktail dress for dinner. She dumped the contents of her suitcases out on the floor, desperately hoping it would appear. She had her shoes. She had her purse. But there was no dress.

"David," she said, "I can't go down to that gorgeous dining room dressed like this."

David nodded. Liv was wearing a light pink, linen dress. Pretty, but much too casual. "Let's go to the front desk and ask if there's a dress shop in town," he suggested.

At the front desk, the clerk thought for a moment. "Well, this little town of ours doesn't have any dress shops. There's a TJ Maxx on Route 647, but I wouldn't guess they'd have what you're looking for. Now, over in Sperryville, there's a nice bridal shop. Maybe they could help you. You'll have to hurry, though. I imagine they probably close at five."

As the grandfather clock in the lobby struck four, Liv and David sprinted to the car. By 4:30, they'd arrived at Pebbles Bridal Shop. It was housed in a large Victorian home with a big, wraparound front porch and it reminded Liv of a wedding cake. When they went inside, David explained the dress situation to the owner and Liv was taken to a dressing room. She began to try on dresses and soon found three that she loved.

"David, you decide. Which one do you like best?"

David grinned and turned to the owner of the shop. "We'll take all three," he said. Then he looked back at Liv, shaking his head. "Is this what life is going to be like with you? A constant adventure?"

Liv shrugged her shoulders and giggled. She had found her Prince Charming.

CHAPTER 6

MIAMI VICES

By October, Liv had settled into her new role as a teacher. Her principal was allowing her to create and teach her own curriculum, and Liv was thrilled at the career path that she had chosen. In preparation for completing her internship, she was beginning to send out résumés to some of the finest schools in the DC area. Best of all, David had told her that he would be more than willing to relocate his business up North. She could have her dream teaching job, and they could both be close to their families in Jersey.

On the Saturday before Columbus Day, Liv got up bright and early to catch the first plane of the day out of the Roanoke–Blacksburg Airport to Miami. Sunday was going to be her twenty-second birthday and David had promised her a weekend full of fun and surprises. Once on the plane, she began daydreaming about what Miami would be like. She'd only seen it on TV in "Miami Vice." She'd spent a lot of time with her family in Palm Beach, and in Naples with Ryan, but she'd never before been to Miami. As the plane touched down, her heart began to race with

18

anticipation. She hadn't seen David since Labor Day. When the plane reached the gate, she practically jumped out of her seat and raced to the baggage claim area. When she arrived at the baggage claim, there was David. God, he was so incredibly handsome, she thought. He stood waiting for her, holding a single red rose. She ran towards him. He grabbed her and passionately kissed her. "Boy, have I missed you," he said.

"Me, too," Liv beamed.

"Well, let's grab your luggage. My car is parked right outside."

Once outside, David walked Liv over to a 1990 yellow Ferrari Testarossa with black interior, opening the door for her.

"Wow, David, is this your car?" Liv remembered David only driving a gray Jeep Laredo growing up. This was definitely a step up.

"Yes. The flower business is doing extremely well. Come on, I want to show you my Miami!"

From the airport, David took the expressway heading east towards the ocean, first swinging through downtown where Liv stared out of the window of the Testarossa at the towering steel and glass office buildings. He drove up Biscayne Boulevard, past the grassy Bayfront Park, and then over the causeway to South Beach. On the causeway, Liv looked out at the blue water towards the Port of Miami where she spotted a row of cruise ships. Once in South Beach, David turned down Collins Avenue. They drove through the Art Deco District. Liv was delighted by the pastel-colored art deco buildings. It seemed as though she'd been transported back in time to the 1940s. The oceanfront was lined with enormous high-rise hotels that screamed glamour and wealth. The opposite side of the street was lined with boutique shops and outdoor cafes with colorful umbrellas. The cafes were the perfect place for the beautiful people of Miami to catch up and take a break from the Florida sunshine.

On the ocean side, a long sidewalk ran between the grass and the beach, full of joggers, dog walkers, and the beautiful people strolling along. There were muscular men, and women in string bikinis, showing off their perfect bodies that had been kissed by the sun. The street was lined with Bentleys, Lamborghinis, and Aston Martins. The area was vibrant and glamorous, and Liv felt as if she was in another world. She definitely wasn't in New Jersey anymore.

Eventually, David spun the car around and headed back across the causeway, around downtown, and ultimately onto Brickell Avenue, lined with condominium towers that faced Biscayne Bay. Finally, David pulled into 1643 Brickell, the Santa Maria building. The Santa Maria was a fifty-one story, all-glass building. Each condo had windows from the floor to the ceiling. Liv thought it looked like a giant glass house. The doorman grabbed Liv's luggage and led her and David into the elevator. The elevator ascended and then opened into David's apartment on the twenty-third floor. The apartment was 3,100 square feet with breathtaking views of the bay and downtown Miami. The apartment had a wraparound balcony, gourmet kitchen, marble flooring, and an exquisite bathroom with an oversized soaking tub. Light streamed in from the windows and the place seemed like something out of a movie.

David gave Liv a tour of his apartment. When they reached the bedroom, he said, "You have no idea how much I've missed you." He reached down and pulled her sundress over her head. She quickly slipped off her shoes and unhooked her bra. David kicked off his loafers and removed his pants and boxers. Then he slid Liv's panties down her legs. He took her hand and led her over to the giant window that overlooked the bay. He stood behind her, taking both of her hands and pressing them firmly over her head against the glass. The glass was warm from the sun. David stood behind her, kissing her neck and grabbing her breasts. He loved how wet she was. He leaned forward and whispered in her ear, "I want you to cum for me." He felt amazing inside of her.

"I'm going to cum for you," she said. "I'm going to cum now!" She had missed making love to him so very much. Afterwards, David led Liv over to his bed and they lay in each other's arms naked. It was so nice to finally be together.

Finally, David got up, saying, "Liv, let's take a quick shower and head down to the pool!" At the pool, he ordered a bottle of Dom Perignon and the seafood tower. He and Liv spent the rest of the day gazing into each other's eyes, soaking up the sun, and relaxing by the pool. It was the perfect day.

After the beautiful day at the pool, Liv decided that she would like to take a relaxing bath before dinner. She filled the tub with very warm water and added some lavender bath salts. She slid into the tub and closed her eyes and let the warm water envelop her. David came into the bathroom wearing a white robe carrying two flutes of champagne. He set down the champagne flutes on the side of the tub and untied his robe. "May I join you?" he said.

"Please do, Mr. Santoro," Liv said.

He slipped into the tub facing Liv. She leaned forward and began kissing him as he caressed her breasts. She kissed his neck and then she climbed on top of him, wanting to make love to her future husband in the tub. She couldn't imagine ever getting tired of making love to him.

Afterwards, David climbed out of the tub and grabbed a towel to wrap Liv up in. They went into the bedroom and laying on the bed was a bright orange dress and platinum gold heels. "Happy birthday," he said. "I thought you might want to wear this to dinner tonight. I have a surprise for you."

David and Liv got dressed for dinner. They then got into the elevator. David leaned forward and kissed her. "You look beautiful tonight." David took Liv's hand and led her through the lobby out to the marina.

"David, where are we going?"

"I have a surprise for you." He led her over to a fifty-foot AMT Black Series cigarette boat. The name on the back of the boat said *Liv Large*. "I bought this boat last week. I thought it might be fun to take it to dinner."

Liv's jaw dropped. "David, have you lost your mind? This is way too much. The car, the condo, the boat. I actually just found out how much my ring cost. David, look me in the eye. Are you sure you can afford all this?"

"Sweetheart, everything is fine. The world is our oyster!" David extended his hand and helped Liv on board. He turned on the large outboard motors and they soon were gliding at lightning speed over the bay. David began to slow down and soon docked the boat at Monty's Raw Bar in Coconut Grove. Monty's was a large, tropical waterfront restaurant with a huge thatched roof. There was a Caribbean band playing and tiki torches everywhere.

David seemed to know everyone in the place. He shook hands and introduced Liv to at least a dozen people. Liv noticed right away the dress of the clientele of the restaurant. The men were handsome in their silk shirts. They wore crisp, light-colored pants and expensive loafers. The women all wore short gorgeous dresses, stylish high heels, and carried fashionable purses. David's acquaintances were all young and they all seemed to have a sophisticated and confident air about them.

The hostess approached David and said, "We have your usual table reserved for you, Mr. Santoro."

David whispered in Liv's ear. "These are one of my best clients. I do all of their flower arrangements." The hostess led them to a table overlooking the bay. The sun was setting and magnificent hues of pink, purple, and orange danced across the sky. David and Liv drank wine, ate oysters, and danced the night away to the sound of the Caribbean band.

At the end of the night, David helped Liv back on board the boat and they headed home, this time much slower, taking in the beautiful Miami skyline. The lights of the tall buildings pierced the velvet black sky. The three-quarter moon shone high above, the light from it glimmering on the ripples of the bay. The air was fresh and clean and Liv loved the way it felt against her face and body. Her head was swirling with the events of the day.

Once back at the condo, David poured himself a glass of Scotch on the rocks, lit a Romeo y Julieta cigar, and stepped out onto the balcony. Liv went into the bathroom, put on a white lingerie outfit and then joined him. They looked into each other's eyes and said nothing. Liv unbuckled his belt and slid her hand inside his pants. She loved how excited he was. She began kissing his neck and unbuttoning his shirt. She kept kissing him as she worked her way down, finally dropping down to her knees. She began kissing and licking him very slowly; she wanted to please him in every way. She then stood and David pulled down the top of her lingerie, exposing her breasts. She reached down and removed her thong. He turned her around, pushing her stomach against the railing. Liv moaned loudly with pleasure. "David, please don't stop! Please!" David reached up and covered Liv's mouth and then came deep inside of her.

David led her back into the bedroom. He pulled the sheets back and they both crawled into bed naked. "Sweet dreams, my angel."

The next day, Liv woke to a dozen flower arrangements in David's bedroom. They were all her favorites—hydrangeas, roses, peonies, in soft white ivory and shades of pink. David entered the bedroom carrying a silver tray. It was Liv's favorite breakfast, eggs Benedict. He placed the tray on the bed, and fed her a bite of breakfast, and then said, "Happy birthday, my love."

They enjoyed a wonderful morning of breakfast in bed followed by hours of making love. Liv went into the bathroom and turned on the shower. David came in and said, "There's something I have to take care of at my office. Don't worry, I'll only be gone for a couple hours. I'll be back around noon to pick you up. I've arranged a spa day for the two of us at the historic Biltmore Hotel." David kissed Liv and then hurried off to work.

After showering, Liv walked into David's dressing room to get ready for the afternoon at the spa. She stared in disbelief at all of David's designer clothes. Growing up, she'd only ever seen him in cut-off Levis and tank tops. She dressed and turned to leave when she noticed that David's large Heritage safe had been left slightly opened. She knew David kept his growing watch collection in the safe. *He was in such a hurry to get to work, he probably forgot to close it*, she thought. She went to swing the door shut but then instead decided to take a peek.

She stood for a moment in a daze, trying to make sense of what she was seeing. There were no watches in the safe. Instead, there were bricks of cocaine and money, stacked from the floor to the ceiling of the safe. For a full minute she took in the contents of the safe. She could hardly believe her eyes. Now everything made sense. Her ring, the car, the condo, the boat. Tears began to roll down her face. *How could he have done this?*

Liv slowly removed her engagement ring and placed it on top of the drugs and money. Then she went into the bedroom and quickly began packing her suitcases. She then called down to the bell stand and ordered a taxi to the airport. Sitting in the back of the cab, she felt numb. How could the man of her dreams be one of the largest drug dealers in Miami?

CHAPTER 7

STAND BY YOUR MAN

Liv finally arrived home. She walked in the front door of her apartment and dropped her keys and luggage on the floor. Exhausted, she collapsed onto her sofa. Then she picked up her phone and called the one person she felt comfortable talking to.

"Happy birthday, Liv!" her mother answered cheerfully. "How do you like Miami? I want to hear everything!"

"I'm not in Miami, Mom. I'm back in Annapolis. Listen, Mom, I have to tell you something."

Liv's mother immediately turned serious. "Liv, what's wrong, honey?"

Liv took a deep breath and told her mother about the events of the weekend.

"Oh, my God, Liv. I'm…stunned. It can't be. I mean, I can't believe David would get himself mixed up in all of that. His family would be devastated, especially his grandmother! He's always been the apple of her eye."

"I know, Mom. And I don't know what to do. I love him more than anything, but I can't be involved in what he's doing."

"I know, Liv, of course not. But look, you can't just walk away from him, either. Not yet. You've known him your entire life. We've all known him. He's always been such a good kid, and we all know how much he loves you!"

"Mom…I just don't know what to do."

"I think you need to give him a choice. Explain to him that he can leave Miami and start a family with you, or…he can stay in Miami and lose you forever. It's really that simple, Liv. The choice is his."

"I don't know, Mom…"

"Tell him you don't need all of those material things. Liv, just explain to him that you want a simple life with him. Listen, Liv, just take some time and think about it. Please."

"Okay, Mom."

"Sweetheart, I'm so very sorry all of this is happening to you. Please try to get some sleep tonight and see how you feel about all of this in the morning. Liv, you know that whatever you decide, I love you."

"I know, Mom. Thanks. I love you, too."

Liv crawled into bed, hugged her pillow, and cried herself to sleep. The next day she went to work, barely able to concentrate. The day seemed to last forever but by the time she got home that evening, she'd made up her mind. Her mother was right. She had to give David a chance to do the right thing. She imagined a lot of women would simply walk away, but that wasn't the kind of woman that she was. She had a bond with David. The fact that they had known each other their whole lives meant something to her. And she knew that underneath it all, David was a good man. She picked up the phone and called him, not even sure of exactly how to begin.

"Hi, David," she started.

"Liv, I'm so sorry. Please let me explain," he said immediately.

"No, David! I just need you to listen. What you're involved in down there—that's not the life I'm looking for. Now, I spoke to my mother last night."

"Oh, my God, Liv. You told your parents?"

"Well, no, just my mom. I can assure you she's not going to tell anyone. First of all, I want you to know I love you and I honestly believe that I'm supposed to spend the rest of my life with you. Now, the way I look at it, you have a choice to make. We can get married, move to Jersey, and you can work for the family business. Or, you can stay down in Miami. And lose me forever! David, it's up to you. What do you want?"

There was a long pause before David finally spoke. "I want *you*, Liv. I want a life with you. Forever. I'm so very sorry!"

Liv started to cry. "I want you, too, David! David, everyone makes mistakes. Let's just try to put this all behind us!"

"Okay. You're right. Just give me this week to get things in order down here. I'll fly up on Friday and we can begin to plan our future. Together. Liv, thanks for standing by me and thanks for giving me another chance. I love you."

"I love you, too. Always."

The rest of the week flew by and when Friday arrived, Liv was thrilled to know she'd be seeing David. They had so much to talk about. It was time to focus on their future and to put this whole mess behind them. Liv was just getting ready to leave for the airport to pick up David when her phone rang. It was her mother.

"Liv, sit down." Her mother's voice was trembling.

"What's wrong, Mom?"

"David's mom just called me."

"Okay…what's going on?"

"Liv, David has been arrested for selling cocaine."

"What? No!! That's impossible."

"Liv, he is being held without bond."

"Oh my God! I have to go to see him."

"Liv, you can't do anything right now. Try to stay calm. I promise to call you back when I know more."

Liv decided to call David's mother.

"Susan, it's Liv. My mother just called me and told me about David."

"Liv," said Susan in a shaky voice, "did you know my son was selling drugs?"

"No! Of course not! I just found out when I was down there for my birthday. I was as shocked as you are! Look, Susan, you know your son, you know the kind of man he really is. He just got mixed up with the wrong people. We had a long talk and he was planning to walk away from everything and everyone down there."

"Well, Liv, he didn't walk away soon enough. He's being held without bond and he's looking at ten years in prison."

"Susan, I need to see him. Please, I'm begging you!"

"Liv, he won't see anyone. He won't even see me." David's mother began to cry. "Liv, how did this happen?"

"I don't know, Susan…I just don't know."

After the phone conversation, Liv suddenly felt ill and ran into the bathroom to throw up.

The next few months were a nightmare. David's case was all over the news. They were calling it the largest cocaine bust in South Florida's history. David continued to refuse to see anyone, including Liv. Finally, the day of his trial came. It went as far as jury selection before David made a plea deal. He decided to surrender the names of his drug partners. For this, he was guaranteed a reduced sentence. Even though he decided to cooperate, he was still looking at four years in prison.

Liv's heart was broken. She couldn't imagine David in prison and a life without him. She decided to write to him. She wrote one letter a week for an entire year, begging to see him. He never responded. She finally gave up. The fairy tale was over. She often wondered if she would ever find happiness again.

CHAPTER 8

OPPOSITES ATTRACT

A year had passed since David had been sentenced to prison. Sadly, Liv had never heard from him. They say time heals all wounds. Liv wasn't sure if that was true. She finally decided that she had no choice but to just move on with her life. She decided to focus all of her energy on her new teaching career and had given up on dating altogether.

That spring, she had graduated from Roanoke with honors and secured her dream job at St. Mary's School in Annapolis, Maryland. She and Buddy moved into a beautiful townhome at 771 Primrose Lane. The townhouse had a huge deck that overlooked a nature preserve and was only minutes from St. Mary's and the historic Annapolis Harbor. She loved Annapolis and was thrilled to be living so close to the water again.

She soon found out that teaching really was her passion. She absolutely adored her kindergarten class. The town of Annapolis was charming with its cobblestone streets, boutique shops, and wonderful restaurants. Meanwhile, the Jersey Shore was only three hours away and she was especially grateful to be able to go home and visit with her family often.

Liv had made many great friends on the school staff, and on January 13, 1993, she and nine fellow teachers purchased a table at the Black Tie and Diamond Gala honoring Wounded Warriors. The event this year was being held at the beautiful Westin Annapolis Hotel. Liv was excited for her girl's night out. She decided to wear a white cocktail dress that was covered in small white pearls and white sequins. At six o'clock, her cab pulled up to the Westin and she met her friends in the lobby. Then they all entered the magnificent ballroom as each of them was handed their table assignment along with a glass of champagne. Liv gazed around at the elegant ballroom and the tables complete with gold tablecloths, crystal stemware, and silver candelabras.

Liv found her place card and then decided to have a look at the silent auction items. She was admiring a set of pearl bracelets when she heard a young gentleman say, "They're almost as beautiful as you are." Liv felt herself blush as she turned around. In front of her stood a stunning young man wearing a Navy dress white uniform. He was six-four, muscular, with light brown hair, piercing blue eyes, and chiseled features. "Hello," he smiled. "Allow me to introduce myself. I'm Cadet Donovan. Kurt Donovan."

"Hi," Liv smiled back. "I'm Olivia Whittaker." Her hands began to sweat. Luckily, the dinner bell rang and the guests were asked to please take their seats. "Well, it was very nice to meet you," Liv said as she turned to head back to her table.

"You as well," Kurt replied.

Back at the table, Liv's girlfriends began to tease her. "Who was that gorgeous god you were talking to?" Liv rolled her eyes and laughed. Her friends knew that she had sworn off men for a while, but Kurt really was quite stunning.

After a lovely dinner, the DJ began to play. Liv and her friends hit the dance floor, doing the electric slide. This is just what Liv needed. It was so nice to have an evening out and to enjoy life again.

When the song ended, the DJ played a slow song. To the opening sounds of Garth Brooks singing "Shameless," Liv felt a tapping on her shoulder.

"May I please have this dance?"

Liv nodded. Kurt took her hand and pulled her close. She felt safe and protected in his arms. She kept thinking of that old saying: *You'll find love when you stop looking.* Was this her next love? Was she ready?

When the song ended, Kurt offered to buy Liv a drink at the bar. Liv agreed and they found a small, private table in the corner to enjoy their cocktails. Kurt told Liv that he was a senior at the Naval Academy, and that he'd been accepted into BUD/S—Basic Underwater Demolition/SEAL school in California. His goal was to one day become a Navy SEAL. She was impressed. Liv told Kurt a little bit about herself, too, how she'd just moved to Annapolis in the fall and was teaching kindergarten at St. Mary's. They made small talk for a while and exchanged phone numbers. Then Liv excused herself to get back to her friends.

"It was very nice to meet you," Kurt said. "Maybe we could go to dinner sometime?"

"Sure, I'd like that," Liv replied.

By the time she returned to her table, everyone was gone. She hadn't realized how late it was. When she looked down at her watch, it showed that it was half past midnight. She grabbed her purse and coat and headed to the front entrance of the hotel to get a taxi. While she was waiting for the taxi, the valet pulled up with Kurt's red Volkswagen Golf GTI. "Can I give you a lift home?" Kurt asked.

"If you don't mind," Liv said.

"Of course not."

As they walked towards the car, the valet opened the door for Liv and remarked, "You two sure make a beautiful couple."

Liv giggled and said, "We just met each other tonight."

"You could have fooled me. You look like you've been together forever. Well, you two have a nice evening."

"Thank you," said Liv.

Soon enough, Kurt pulled up in front of Liv's townhome. She looked down at her hands folded in her lap. She really wanted to ask him to come in, but was she ready? All of a sudden, she blurted out, "Would you like to come in?" There was no turning back now.

"That sounds nice," Kurt said, parking the car. Once inside, Liv excused herself and went into her bedroom. She quickly threw on a pair of sweats. *Now what?* she thought. When she returned to the living room, Kurt had taken off his jacket. His white undershirt showed off his muscular physique and huge biceps. *Oh, boy, what have I gotten myself into?* Liv suddenly felt extremely nervous. She wasn't quite sure what to do next. She decided that cooking a late-night snack would ease her nerves and would give them a chance to get to know each other better.

"You know, I'm kinda hungry for some reason," she said.

Kurt laughed. "Well, I'm always hungry."

"What if I make us some pasta?"

"Sounds great!"

Liv went into the kitchen and started cooking. Then she set the kitchen table, lit some candles, and poured two glasses of wine. "The pasta's all ready. Let's eat."

Kurt sat down at the table and took a bite of the pasta. "Olivia Whittaker, you're amazing. It's the middle of the night and you go into the kitchen and whip this up! Incredible!"

"Thank you," Liv smiled. "I'm glad you like it. It's one of my specialties. Spinach pasta. I really love to cook."

"Well you can cook for me anytime! I'll tell you what, if we were married, I'd like to have this once a week. But if I'm being completely honest, I don't think I'm ever getting married. I just don't feel that a career in the Navy and marriage work, you know? Just think about it. There's too much time apart and you're constantly moving. It's very stressful, even for the best marriages. So I've decided to be content with serving my country and traveling the world. What about you, Olivia? Do you want to get married one day?"

"Well, first of all, please call me Liv. That's what my friends and family call me. And yes, I love children and I definitely hope that one day I'll have a family of my own."

Kurt raised his glass and said, "Cheers to new friends. May all of our dreams come true! Liv, I'm really glad I met you."

"Me, too," said Liv.

After their late-night snack, Kurt helped Liv clean up. Then he put on his jacket and Liv walked him to the door. He kissed her on the cheek and said, "I had a great time tonight. Thank you."

"I had a great time, too."

Liv watched Kurt get into his car. She waved goodbye. As she watched him drive away, the strangest thought entered her mind: *That's the man I'm going to marry.* She smiled and went back into the house. For the first time in ages, she slept soundly that night.

When Liv returned home from work on Monday, there was a small box with a note at her front door.

The note read, "Can I please take you to dinner this week? —Kurt."

Liv smiled and opened the box. It was the set of pearl bracelets from the auction. Had Liv finally found her husband?

CHAPTER 9

VALENTINE'S DAY

Over the next month, Liv found herself spending more and more time with Kurt. They had weekly dinner dates, they went to the movies, and went bowling. Every Sunday, Kurt came over to do his laundry and Liv would make them dinner. She loved every second that she spent with him.

On Valentine's Day, she came home from work to find a giant bouquet of red roses at her door. The card read: *"Liv, Happy Valentine's Day! —Kurt."* She grabbed the phone and called to thank him for the thoughtful flowers.

"I'm glad you like them, Liv. Listen, I thought maybe this Sunday, instead of you cooking, you would let me take you out to dinner."

"I'd love that," Liv said.

"Great. I'll pick you up around 6:30."

"Perfect."

But when Liv put the phone down, she suddenly found herself confused. Kurt Donovan had told her he definitely didn't want to get married and have a family. But why was he spending all this time with someone who was just a friend? And what about the pearl brace-lets and the roses? Do you send a friend red roses on Valentine's Day?

The next day at school, Liv decided to confide in another teacher. She had become close to Debbie Taylor. "Debbie, I really need your advice," she said.

"Sure. What's going on?"

"Well, you know that Kurt and I are spending all this time together. He even sent me roses for Valentine's Day."

"Okay. That's nice. So what's the problem?"

"Well, I don't know if he just wants to be friends or if he wants to be, you know, something more."

Debbie looked thoughtful. "Hmm...well, you know, Liv, there's really only one way to find out."

"What?"

"Ask him."

"Just *ask* him? Just like that?"

"Sure. Just say, 'Kurt, I really like spending time with you, but are we just friends, or maybe something more?'"

"Well, I guess I could say that. He's supposed to take me to dinner on Sunday."

"There you go. The perfect chance. When he comes over to pick you up, invite him in for a glass of wine and ask him. At least then you'll know where you stand."

"Okay," nodded Liv. "I'll do it."

That Sunday, Liv was a complete wreck. She nervously got ready, dressing in a navy blue, pleated skirt outfit; 6:30 couldn't arrive fast enough. Finally, the doorbell rang. There was Kurt, wear-ing his leather bomber jacket, white T-shirt, and jeans. *Damn, he is sexy,* she thought.

"Come on in," said Liv. "I thought we could have a glass of wine before dinner."

"Sounds great," said Kurt. "I made a reservation for us at that new Chinese restaurant that just opened. The Dragon."

"Sounds perfect," Liv said as she poured two glasses of Zinfandel. Then they both sat down on the couch. Liv had rehearsed what she'd planned to say, but before she could get a word out, Kurt pulled a small box from his pocket.

"You told me how much you love Valentine's Day," he said, "so I decided to get you a little something. Actually, I never celebrated this holiday before I met you. I really hope you like it."

Liv opened the box. In it was a small gold rope bracelet. Kurt put his wine glass down. "Let me put it on you," he said.

Liv looked down at the bracelet on her wrist, now feeling more confused than ever.

Kurt noticed her expression. "Oh, you don't like it. No problem. We can take it back. I can get you something else."

"No, no, no," Liv said. "It's not that. I love the bracelet. I'm just... confused."

"Confused? Confused about what?"

Liv looked down at her hands. "I'm confused about your feelings towards me." She looked up into his piercing blue eyes. Kurt put his wine glass down. He put his hand on her cheek and kissed her. Then he took off his jacket and his shirt. He laid down on top of her. He reached down and removed her panties. In a moment, he was inside of her. She wrapped her legs tightly around him. He picked her up while he was still inside of her and carried her to the bed.

For the next few hours, Liv had the wildest sex of her life. Afterwards, she got up and brought back two glasses of water. She handed Kurt a glass.

She took a sip. "So, I guess you kinda like me a little?" she said, giggling.

"Yes, Liv, I most definitely like you," Kurt said. He leaned over and kissed her. They both laughed. "Let's order Chinese food."

"That sounds wonderful."

They ended up having dinner in bed and making love all night. As Liv closed her eyes to finally get some rest, she was struck by a thought. *I guess opposites really do attract. But can they last?*

CHAPTER 10

AN OFFICER AND A GENTLEMAN

Kurt and Olivia were like two comets streaking across the sky. They couldn't get enough of each other. They saw each other practically every day. On the weekends, Kurt would just show up at Liv's door, she would jump into his car, and off they'd go. They never had a plan. They would just drive and discover new places and things together.

Liv had no idea if what she was feeling was love or lust, but she was having so much fun that she really didn't care. She remembered a story that her grandmother had told her once. Liv's grandmother, Dovey, was dating a very nice boy named Stanley in high school. He came from a good family, had perfect manners, and was an excellent ballroom dancer. Stanley was a true gentleman through and through. Most likely, this was the young man that Dovey would marry. But then fate stepped in. One day, Dovey was walking home from school when a boy named William threw a snowball at her and then ran up and shoved her into a snowbank. Dovey had told Liv that it was love at first sight. "Sometimes, Liv, love just doesn't make sense," her grandmother had said.

Dovey had a choice to make. Stick with Stanley and have a very safe and predictable life, or throw caution to the wind and be on a wild roller coaster ride with William for the rest of her life. She chose William, Liv's grandfather, and never regretted it for one second. Remembering this story, Liv decided not to question her relationship with Kurt. Instead, she decided to put her seatbelt on and enjoy the ride, not quite knowing where she'd end up.

At the beginning of April, Liv asked her mother if it would be okay if she brought Kurt home for Easter. She wanted him to meet her family and to see where she grew up. Liv's mom was hesitant at first. She didn't want to see her daughter's heart broken again. But she knew that bringing Kurt home meant a lot to Liv and she wanted to be supportive. And so she agreed.

On Good Friday, Kurt and Liv headed to the Jersey Shore. After driving over the Point Pleasant Bridge, Liv pointed out the Barnegat Bay, Brave New World Surf Shop, Hoffman's Ice Cream, the original Jersey Mike's sub shop, and the boardwalk. These were some of the places Point Pleasant Beach, New Jersey was most known for. She was excited to show Kurt her hometown. Soon, they pulled into her parent's driveway and walked up to the front door where Liv's mom was waiting to greet them.

"Mom, this is Kurt," said Liv.

"It's very nice to meet you, Mrs. Whittaker," smiled Kurt. "Thanks for having me for the weekend."

"Well, it's nice to meet you too, Kurt. Liv, please show Kurt to the guest room so he can get settled." There was no sharing of beds in the Whittaker home unless there was a wedding band on one's finger. Liv took Kurt on a tour of the house and then showed him to his room.

That evening, Liv's parents took them all out to dinner to the Manasquan River Country Club. Kurt and Liv's father, Peter, seemed to hit it off immediately. They talked about sports, politics, and the military. Liv's mother noticed throughout the evening, whether they were walking across the room, sitting at the dinner table, or driving in the car, that Kurt always held Liv's hand. She definitely liked how affectionate he was towards her daughter, and the chemistry between them seemed electric. Liv was beaming and her mother thought how nice it was to see her daughter happy once again.

On Easter morning, everyone dressed for church. Kurt decided to wear his Navy dress whites. The sight of him in his uniform took Liv's breath away. After the Easter service at All Saints Church in Bay Head, they headed over to the Bluffs Restaurant on the ocean to meet up with the rest of Liv's family. As they pulled into the restaurant's parking lot, Liv's grandparents pulled in at the same time.

"My grandparents," Liv whispered to Kurt.

Liv's grandfather stepped out of his Lincoln Town Car, buttoned his long camel hair coat, and placed his wool fedora on his head. Liv watched as Kurt jumped out of the car and walked right over to her grandfather, shaking his hand and introducing himself. Then he stepped over to the passenger side and opened the door for Dovey. He extended his arm and escorted her up to the entrance of the restaurant. Inside, all of Liv's cousins, aunts, and uncles were already seated around the table. Liv introduced everyone to Kurt who smiled broadly and nodded politely at each person. His charisma and charm were impossible to resist. It was very clear that Liv's entire family was very impressed with Kurt Donovan.

Liv's grandmother insisted that Kurt sit next to her, and after brunch, she pulled Liv aside. "So, you decided to get on the roller coaster ride, I see," she grinned. Liv giggled. "Good for you," her grandmother continued. "He's so incredibly handsome, and very charming."

"Thanks," Liv said, hugging her grandmother and then squeezing her hands. Her grandmother's approval meant everything to her.

That evening, as Kurt and Liv drove back to Annapolis, Liv reflected on the weekend. She couldn't imagine that it could have gone any better. Her family had truly embraced Kurt, which was a pleasant surprise. As she stared out the window of the car, with Kurt holding her hand, she couldn't help but wonder if she might be holding hands with her future husband.

CHAPTER 11

GRADUATION DAY

It was May 22nd, Kurt's graduation day from the Naval Academy. Liv ran out the door in a lavender dress that she had picked up at Ann Taylor's the day before. She didn't want to miss one second of Kurt's graduation.

When she arrived at the Marine Corps Stadium in Annapolis, she wasn't prepared for the crowd. Over 30,000 people gathered in the stadium to watch the graduation. It was beyond moving, and she was so very proud of Kurt. Only one cadet from the Naval Academy was chosen that year to go through BUD/S. It was quite an amazing accomplishment.

After the graduation, she waded through the crowd until she finally found Kurt. He was taking pictures with his family. This was the first time that she would be meeting them. As soon as he spotted her, he ran towards her, picked her up, and kissed her. He took her hand and said, "Liv, come and meet my family."

They walked over and Kurt introduced her to his grandparents, Fred and Mary, and then to his mother, Lisa.

Liv immediately hugged all of them. Kurt's grandfather said,

"It's so nice to finally meet you. We've heard such nice things."

Kurt's mother said, "We were hoping that you would join us tonight for dinner to celebrate Kurt's graduation."

"I would really like that. Of course I'll come to dinner," Liv said, smiling.

His grandfather pulled out his camera and said, "Let's get a few pictures of you two."

After taking a bunch of pictures, Kurt walked Liv to her car. "Thanks so much for coming today."

"It was amazing," she said. "I'm so incredibly proud of you."

"I'll pick you up for dinner tonight around seven?"

"Sounds perfect."

"We're going to the Chart House."

"Great!"

Kurt kissed her and then ran back to join his family.

At seven, Kurt and Liv were in the car and heading to the restaurant. Liv was a little nervous. She really wanted Kurt's family to like her. "Your family seems very sweet."

"My grandparents are the best. My grandfather was in the Army and my grandmother was a military nurse. My grandfather was injured in World War II and my grandmother ended up being his nurse. That's how they met. My grandfather said it was love at first sight.

"Liv, I guess I should tell you a little bit more about my mom. My mom had me when she was very young. She was actually still in high school. She got pregnant with me in her senior year and had to drop out. I've never even met my father; he left before I was born. So basically, my grandparents are more like parents to me. They're the ones who really raised me. I don't know where I'd be without them. That's why my graduation is such a big deal to them, because I'm the first person in our family to graduate from college."

This time, Liv reached over for Kurt's hand. "Thanks for telling me all that. I think I'm even more impressed with you now than I was before." She kissed his hand.

Over dinner, Liv learned a lot more about Kurt and his family. They lived in Asheville, North Carolina. His mother was a bank teller and his grandparents were both retired. They told many stories about Kurt, how he played on every varsity team in high school, how he had straight A's all through high school and was the class valedictorian. He also won the state spelling bee his sophomore year. In his junior year, he had decided he wanted more than anything to become a Navy SEAL. He began running and swimming daily to get ready for the rigorous training that was ahead. You could see the pride on his family's faces as they told the stories. Liv was happy to be included in such a special evening.

After dinner, they said their goodbyes. Liv thanked them for a wonderful dinner. When they got into the car, Kurt said, "Let's take a drive. I really don't feel like going home yet."

"Okay, whatever you want. It's your night."

Kurt drove to the Naval Academy Golf Course.

"Kurt, what are we doing at a golf course at this time of night?" asked Liv.

"Come on." Kurt took Liv's hand and helped her up onto the hood of his car. Then he sat down next to her. "Liv, will you look at all the stars?"

He was right. The sky was full of stars on that crystal clear night in May. Kurt leaned over and began kissing her. He reached up under her skirt and pushed her panties aside. He jumped off the hood of the car and slid her towards him. He removed her panties, then he removed his pants. She threw her legs around his neck. She knew she would always remember this night, making love on the hood of a car under a thousand stars. *Wow!* she thought.

After their golf course adventure, Kurt drove her home.

"Do you want to come in?" Liv said. "I have some champagne in the fridge."

"I really want to, but my family has an early flight home tomorrow and I'm taking them to the airport, so I better not."

"Okay, I understand. We'll have the champagne another time. Thanks again for including me in such a special day." They kissed and said goodnight.

"I'll call you tomorrow," he said.

As he drove away, she suddenly felt sad. He was leaving to start BUD/S on Monday. There were no words to describe how much she was going to miss him.

The next day, Liv heard honking outside of her townhouse. She looked out the window. It was Kurt in a gray Toyota Tacoma pickup truck. *What on earth?* she thought. She ran outside. "Kurt, what is this?"

"I decided to trade in my Volkswagen for this. I'm going to need it to load up all of my stuff and drive across the country."

"Well, I guess you're right," she said.

"Look, I have to pack up and move out of my dorm today. Do you think I could stay here with you tonight?"

"Of course."

"It shouldn't take long. A lot of the guys are helping me."

"Okay. What if I make spaghetti pie for us for dinner?"

"You know that's one of my favorites."

"Great! Just come over as soon as you're done."

Liv went to work in the kitchen assembling the spaghetti pie—angel hair pasta, ricotta cheese, Italian sausage, Prego sauce, all topped with mozzarella cheese. She also decided to make garlic bread and a Caesar salad. She gathered a bunch of candles and placed them all around her townhouse. She set the table and put on some Frank Sinatra. She decided to wear a very long, sheer white, lace dress. As she finished dressing, there was a knock at the door. She opened the door.

"Wow, look at you," said Kurt as he kissed her. He took her hand and they went up the stairs. "Dinner smells amazing."

"Everything's ready. Can you please open the wine?"

"Of course."

She put the spaghetti pie on the table with the garlic bread and then tossed the Caesar salad. As they sat across the table from each other, she couldn't help but wonder if this was their last dinner together. Her eyes began to tear up. Kurt got up.

"Liv, please don't do this." He kissed her. "I really don't want tonight to be sad."

"I know," she said. She wiped away her tears. "I'm sorry."

"Let's enjoy this night," Kurt said. "Okay?"

"Okay."

After dinner, she went into her bedroom and put on a red lace lingerie outfit. Kurt was in the kitchen cleaning up. He turned around.

"You're beautiful," he said. "Just like the first time I saw you." He scooped her up in his arms and carried her to the bedroom. They made love all night.

As the sun began to rise and beams of sunlight came through her blinds, Kurt leaned over and said, "I have to get going. It's a long drive."

"I know." A single tear ran down her cheek. He wiped it away. She put on her robe and walked him to his truck. "Please drive safe."

"I will." He leaned out the window and kissed her one last time. As he drove away, her stomach dropped. She could honestly say she had no idea if she would ever see Kurt Donovan again, but it had been one hell of a ride.

CHAPTER 12

THE ROLLER COASTER RIDE

Almost one week had passed since Kurt had left for California. Unfortunately, Liv hadn't heard from him. It was Sunday morning and she decided to take Buddy for a long walk through the nature preserve to take her mind off things. But on her walk, she couldn't help but think about all of those wonderful Sundays and weekends with Kurt. This weekend was very different—no weekend adventures, no romantic sleepovers, and no Sunday dinners. Liv had come to the conclusion that out of all of the human emotions, missing someone for her, was by far the worst. And in her life, she had become all too familiar with missing that special someone.

When Liv and Buddy returned to the townhouse, the phone was ringing. Liv dropped Buddy's leash and ran to pick up the phone. "Hello?" she said.

"Well, hello there, stranger," said the voice on the other end.

Kurt's voice. Suddenly Liv's heart was racing a thousand miles an hour.

"Liv, I'm so sorry I haven't called sooner," he continued. "They're keeping me really busy out here. Five a.m. wake-up calls,

PT, beach and pool drills. And they only give us fifteen minutes to eat all of our meals. I'm not going to lie; it's really been tough. But I do like the guys in my class a lot. So, I have a question to ask you."

"Okay," Liv said.

"Well, they're giving us a long weekend for the Fourth of July, and I was hoping you'd want to come out here to visit me. Have you ever been to California?"

"No, I've never been."

"I think you'll love it. But there are a few things you need to know: because we're not married, you can't stay on base with me. I did find a beautiful hotel up the road called the Hotel Del Coronado. I run by it every morning. I thought I could get us a room there with my military discount. So, the question is, Liv, will you come visit me?"

"Oh, my gosh, yes, I would love to, Kurt. Of course!"

"Great! We'll plan on it. Now, just so you know, I can't call you as often as I would like because of this intense training schedule, but I thought I'd write you a letter a week, if that's okay."

"Yes, I'd really like that."

"Great. Okay, well, I really do have to go now. I'll write you this week and I'll call you again as soon as I can. And, Liv…I really miss you!"

"I miss you, too! See you soon."

"Can't wait!"

They said their goodbyes and hung up, and as Liv held the receiver in her hand, she smiled and thought to herself, "Well, I guess the rollercoaster ride isn't over!"

CHAPTER 13

CALIFORNIA DREAMING

It was the Thursday before the Fourth of July. Liv was on a Continental flight out of BWI bound for San Diego. She was beyond nervous and excited. She tried to read her book on the plane, *The Bridges of Madison County*, but her mind kept wandering. As the plane flew over the Grand Canyon, the pilot pointed out the view. Liv looked out of her window at the red mountains and found the scene below her to be absolutely breathtaking. She'd seen pictures, but to fly over the Grand Canyon was something she'd never forget. This was a great start to her first trip to California.

After almost six hours on the plane, the pilot put on the FASTEN SEATBELT sign and they began their descent. Liv noticed the small airport below them, seemingly in the middle of the city, and closed her eyes. *There certainly isn't much room for error,* she thought, but the plane touched down smoothly. *Thank God.*

Liv made her way to the baggage claim area. The airport was small, hot, and crowded. Finally, she saw Kurt. He was wearing flip-flops, khaki shorts, and a very tight navy blue T-shirt. Right away, she noticed that he had shaved his head and had lost a lot of weight. She gave him a big hug and kissed him.

"Wow," she said, "You've been working hard out here, I see."

"Yeah, the daily workouts are brutal. I've lost almost 45 pounds since I've been out here. I'm down to 175 pounds."

"Jesus...well, you still look very handsome."

"Thanks. Are you ready to see San Diego?"

"I can't wait!"

Kirk grabbed Liv's bags and they headed towards his truck. They drove through downtown San Diego and then over the Coronado Bridge. Liv was speechless. The bay was full of boats and the mountains touched the sea, something she'd never seen before. Coronado was this perfect seaside town, with its quaint main street and romantic seaside cottages. Liv was immediately taken in by the charm of this tiny island and could definitely see herself living here.

Kurt said, "Let's go to the hotel first and then I'll show you the base."

"Kurt, I'm so excited. I want to see everything! I can hardly believe I'm here."

When they pulled up to the hotel, Liv could hardly believe her eyes. It was a very grand Victorian-style hotel that was white with red-peaked roofs. There was a line of surrey bicycles out front for the guests to enjoy. When she stepped into the hotel, it was like going back in time. The hotel was built in 1888. There was a piano player in the lobby. Liv was in awe of the intricate woodwork in the ceiling and main staircase. The crystal chandeliers were exquisite. This certainly was a magical place. Kurt and Liv checked in at the front desk and then stepped into the hotel's old-fashioned gold elevator, complete with an elevator operator and cage-style metal doors.

Kurt had booked a very sweet corner room with rosebud wallpaper and a four-post bed. Liv was in heaven. She walked in and went immediately to the windows, opening all of them. The views and the smell of the ocean were magnificent. Kurt walked up behind Liv and hugged her.

He whispered into her ear, "Liv, I've been missing you. I want you to know I haven't been with anyone else."

She turned around, looking into his beautiful green eyes. "Really?"

"Yes, really." He kissed her. She went over to the bed. She couldn't wait to make love to him. She pulled off his shirt and unbuttoned his pants. Every fiber of her wanted this man. They spent the rest of the afternoon making love to the sounds of the crashing Pacific Ocean and the seagulls.

Afterwards, Kurt said, "Why don't you get dressed and then we can head on over to the base. I'll show you around and then we can go grab some dinner. I made a reservation at the Chart House because I know how much you like it." Liv kissed Kurt and then went into the bathroom to get ready for dinner.

Downstairs, in front of the hotel, the valet pulled Kurt's truck around, and in less than two minutes, Kurt and Liv were pulling into the Naval Amphibious Base. Kurt took out his military ID card and the guard waved them through the gates. Kurt parked in front of the barracks, a two-story building that reminded Liv of an old dormitory. "Come on," Kurt said, "I'll show you my room."

Kurt unlocked his door and opened it to reveal a small living room with a couch, coffee table, and an old TV. There was a small blue-tiled bathroom with a shower, sink, and toilet. His bedroom had a queen-sized bed with two nightstands and a dresser. There were a stack of clothes and towels folded on the bed. "Oh, the maids must have come."

"Maids?"

"I guess that probably sounds strange. They clean our rooms and do our laundry for us because we just don't have the time. Make yourself at home. I'm going to take a quick shower and then we can head out to dinner."

Liv sat down on Kurt's bed. She noticed a picture of the two of them from graduation on his nightstand. She picked up the picture and took in the room. She could hardly believe she was sitting on Kurt's bed.

Shortly, Kurt came out of the bathroom. "Well, what do you think of the base?"

"Kurt, you have no idea how happy I am to be here with you."

He leaned over and kissed her. "Let's go get dinner, okay?"

"I'm all yours. Let's go."

At the Chart House, the hostess showed them to a beautiful window table with a view of the bay and the spectacular sunset. When the waitress came, Liv ordered a Kendall Jackson Chardonnay and Kurt ordered a Corona. The waitress returned with their drinks and they placed their dinner orders.

Kurt took a sip of his beer. "Liv, I should probably warn you, I'll probably be drunk after this one beer. Believe it or not, I haven't had a drink since that last night with you in Annapolis. You might have to carry me back to the hotel."

"Well, luckily we're just across the street from the hotel, so I think we're okay." They both laughed.

The waitress brought out the dinners. Liv took a few bites of her seafood pasta and then glanced over at Kurt. His plate was already empty. "Kurt! Oh my gosh, you must have been starving!"

"No," he laughed. "I'm so sorry. I need to work on my table manners. Remember, I told you that we're only given a short period of time to eat our meals, so I'm used to eating super fast. I'm really sorry."

Liv giggled. "It's fine. But I think you'd better order dessert!"

"You know what, I think I will!"

After dinner, Kurt took Liv back to the hotel. He walked her to her room and then took a seat on the end of the bed. "Liv, listen, I can't stay with you tonight. You know I want to. But we have beach drills early in the morning. It's just for tonight." He added, kissing her, "I can stay with you for the rest of the weekend."

"Don't worry, I understand," Liv replied.

"And, hey, if you happen to be up around six, you'll see me running by on the beach carrying logs."

"Logs?"

"It's part of our morning drills."

"That sounds awful!"

"It kinda is. But I'm getting used to it."

Liv walked him to the door. "Sleep well."

"You too. I'll see you tomorrow."

He kissed her goodnight then she went into the bathroom and got ready for bed. She put on her pajamas and slipped under the sheets, leaving the windows open so she could hear the ocean and smell the crisp, salty night air. She was so happy that she had decided to make this trip and couldn't wait to see what Kurt had planned for the rest of the weekend.

The next morning, Liv rolled over, opened her eyes, and saw the time on the nightstand clock. It was 8:15. She'd slept much longer than she'd expected. She picked up the phone and called down to room service, ordering two poached eggs, whole wheat toast, and a large pot of coffee with extra cream. Then she got up, brushed her teeth, and washed her face. She put on the hotel robe that was hanging on the back of the door and then went over to look out the windows. It was a beautiful California day. Not a cloud in the sky.

Shortly, there was a knock at the door. It was room service.

"Good morning," said the room service attendant.

"Good morning. I was wondering if you could set up breakfast in front of the window."

"Of course. You should enjoy the view. Is this your first time in California?"

"Yes."

"Well, I hope it won't be your last."

"Me too." She signed the bill and then sat down to enjoy her breakfast. After breakfast, she decided to go on a long beach walk. Kurt told her that he wouldn't be back to the hotel until around six. So she had all day to explore Coronado.

The beach was so different than the Jersey Shore. She couldn't get over how the mountains touched the sea. She noticed right away that the sand was much darker and coarser than Jersey. She went and put her toes in the sea. The water was very chilly. She guessed it was probably in the fifties. So, the air coming off the ocean was quite cold. The weather reminded her of a crisp fall day at the Jersey Shore. She soon noticed an obstacle course that was set up on the beach. She stopped and stared at it then looked back at the ocean. She could see a tiny island in the distance. She imagined Kurt training every day on this beach. She was starting to get an idea what his life was like out here. She wondered if this was what he really wanted. And if he was truly happy.

She decided to turn around and head back to the hotel. In the afternoon, she took a surrey ride all around the island. Coronado was very beautiful and very romantic.

At 6:15, Kurt knocked on her hotel room door. "Hi," he smiled. "How was your day?"

"Wonderful," Liv replied. "It's so beautiful here. But I missed you."

"I missed you, too. But now we have the whole weekend. I made reservations for tonight in the Gaslamp District at this restaurant called Nolen. I think you're really going to like it."

"Sounds great. Am I dressed okay?"

"Beautiful, as always."

They got in the car and before long, Kurt pulled up in front of Nolen. They made their way to the rooftop where the hostess led them past a firepit in the middle of the restaurant to a table that overlooked the whole city. "Wow. Kurt, this is amazing!" said Liv.

"I thought you'd like it."

"I mean really amazing. Thank you."

"Thank *you*," Kurt smiled, looking into her eyes. "For being here." He reached across the table and held her hands.

When the waitress came, they ordered drinks and dinner and when the dinner came, Kurt said, "Don't worry; I'm going to eat very slowly tonight." They both laughed. "So tell me, what did you do today?"

"Well, I actually slept pretty late. For me, anyway. Then I ate breakfast and took a long walk on the beach. I saw the obstacle course, by the way."

"Yeah, that's not exactly one of my favorite things."

"I also saw a little island."

"Oh, yeah. They make us swim out there all the time. It's known for having a lot of sharks around it."

Liv put her fork down and folded her hands. "Kurt...may I ask you a question?"

"Sure, anything."

"Are you happy out here?" Now Kurt put his fork down. "Liv, I won't say I'm happy. I'm cold, wet, and sandy most of time. I'm also not very fond of getting tied up and thrown in a pool every day, getting screamed at, and being mentally and physically exhausted all the time. Liv, I don't know how to explain this to you. I've always enjoyed a challenge, and to me this is a huge challenge. Being a SEAL means you are the best of the best. It's a very elite group and I'm also very proud to serve my country. I hope that makes sense."

"Sure. It's your passion."

"Yes, Liv, but it's also who I am."

After dinner, they walked around for a bit, taking in the historic Victorian buildings and streets that were lined with gas lamp streetlights. When they got back to the hotel, Kurt took off his clothes and got into bed. He patted the bed. "Come here. I've really missed you." Liv took her clothes off and joined him. "I want to ask you something, Liv." Kurt sat up and took his dog tags off and placed them over her neck. "Liv, the first night I met you, my buddies were teasing me about you."

"They were? Why?"

"Because, Liv, you're not the kind of girl that you just fool around with. You're the kind of girl that you marry. So, like I told you, I'm not 100 percent sold on this idea of marriage, but I do really care for you a lot and I was hoping you'd agree to be my girlfriend."

Liv looked down at the dog tags between her breasts. She then looked into Kurt's eyes and kissed him. "Make love to me," she said.

That night before going to sleep, Kurt reached over and grabbed her hand. "I love you," he said.

"I love you, too."

That night, he held her hand all night as she slept.

The next day, Kurt showed Liv around La Jolla. She was amazed at the way in which the houses of La Jolla were built into the side of the mountain. She did find the narrow mountain roads terrifying, but the town of La Jolla was beautiful. After a day of sightseeing, they decided to have dinner at the Marine Room. The sea crashed below them as they ate. This was turning out to be a perfect weekend.

For the Fourth of July, they had decided to stay at the hotel and watch the fireworks from the beach. Kurt had asked the hotel to make a beach picnic basket for them. He laid the blanket out, poured some champagne, and set out the food. *How romantic,* Liv thought. And the fireworks were the best she had ever seen in her life, putting her neighborhood fireworks back in Jersey to shame.

The morning after, they ordered room service before heading to the airport. Kurt poured the coffee. "Liv, I have to tell you something. We don't get any time off until Christmas. So, I won't be able to come and visit you."

"I understand," Liv assured him.

"But, listen, I know we can make this work. You don't go back to teaching until September. I was hoping you could come back in August. And then you get long holiday weekends in September and October. I know this is a lot to ask, but I promise to come home for Christmas. So, what do you think?"

Liv got up from the table and sat on his lap. "I think I love you, Kurt Donovan." She kissed him. "That sounds like the perfect plan."

"I love you, too."

Later that morning, staring out of the window of the plane as it took off, Liv watched the mountains fading in the distance. She couldn't help but smile. She thought about the weekend. She thought about Kurt. And she knew she couldn't wait to come back!!

CHAPTER 14

AN INDECENT PROPOSAL

A nd so for the next few months, Liv kept her promise to visit Kurt as often as possible. During her visit in August, Kurt took her to Tijuana. She had never experienced anything like it in her life—dirt roads, chickens roaming around; she even rode on a donkey that was painted to look like a zebra. Kurt persuaded her to do a tequila popper. She was spun around in a barber's chair, turned upside down, and then tequila was poured in her mouth. Talk about a wild ride!

In September, Kurt took her to Universal Studios for the day. On the way back to Coronado, they drove down the Pacific Highway and stopped to have dinner in Malibu at Neptune's Net. Liv loved it! Picnic tables, seafood, and they watched as the sun slowly dipped down into the Pacific! Wonderful.

In October, Kurt surprised Liv for her birthday with a trip to Beverly Hills. They stayed at the Nikko Hotel. It was a modern, upscale hotel in the heart of Beverly Hills. Kurt arranged for a limo tour of the movie stars' homes at night. Liv was excited to see Lucille Ball's home. She had been a huge fan of the *I Love Lucy* show her whole life!

SAMANTHA DUPREE

Each visit with Kurt was better than the one before. Then, Kurt asked Liv to spend Thanksgiving with him. He couldn't leave San Diego because he only got Thanksgiving Day off. Liv was torn. She'd never been away from her family on Thanksgiving. But the thought of Kurt being alone was heartbreaking. She decided to call her mom, telling her of her mixed feelings.

"Mom, what do you think?" she asked.

"Liv, I've been quiet about your relationship with Kurt, but your father and I are very concerned."

"Concerned? Why?"

"Well, you're spending all of your money to go out and see him once a month without any sort of a commitment."

"Mom, I told you we're not seeing other people. We have a wonderful relationship. Mom, I think you and Dad worry too much. And besides, I'm really happy. Doesn't that count for something?"

"Well then, Liv, it sounds like you've already made up your mind about Thanksgiving."

"Yes, Mom, I have. I really hope you and the rest of the family will understand."

"I'll just miss you, Liv. We all will."

"I know, Mom, I'll miss you, too. I love you."

"I love you too."

On Thanksgiving morning, Kurt and Liv drove over to the Fisherman's Wharf to walk around and have an early lunch. They had decided to have Thanksgiving dinner in the Crown Room back at the hotel. When they got to the Fish Market they grabbed an outdoor table to take in the view. But in the back of Liv's mind was the phone conversation she'd had with her mother. Was she really wasting her time and money going to visit Kurt every month? Was this relationship going anywhere? Or was it just fun? Finally, she decided she needed to say something.

60

"Kurt, listen, I had a serious talk with my mom before coming out here and, well, the bottom line is, she got me thinking about us. Now I know when we first met, you told me you really didn't see yourself ever getting married. So…my question to you is, do you still feel the same way?"

"Liv, to be honest, I can't think about anything right now except finishing BUD/S. That's my main focus. And I don't think you should allow yourself to be influenced by other people. I mean, I really like your parents, but we're happy. Isn't that good enough?"

"You're right," Liv said, managing a smile. "Of course. I'm sorry. I shouldn't have said anything. It's just been on my mind and, well, this is the first Thanksgiving that I haven't been with my family."

Kurt reached across the table and took Liv's hand. "I know, and I'm so thankful that you came out here. We're going to have a great Thanksgiving. I promise." He leaned across the table and kissed her.

When they got back to the hotel, Liv told Kurt she wanted to take a walk on the beach before dinner.

"Is everything all right?" he said. "I'll come with you."

"No, no, everything's fine. I just want to be by myself for a little. I'll be back in forty-five minutes." Then she kissed him on the cheek, grabbed her hotel key, and headed to the beach. Beach walks always cleared her head.

The sun was setting and it was beautiful, but Liv found herself feeling more and more upset. *What does he think I'm just supposed to do? Keep flying out here forever with no promise of anything?* She kept walking, trying to calm herself down. *It's Thanksgiving, after all,* she thought. *I left my entire family to be out here with him. I must be crazy!*

She decided to pray. She stopped and looked up at the sky. She saw the first evening star. *God, I just need your help.* Then she thought, *If it's meant to be, it will be.* She breathed in the salt air and headed back to the hotel. She decided to make the best of the situation and was determined to have a nice Thanksgiving.

For dinner, Liv wore a cranberry pantsuit with gold buttons and Kurt wore his Navy dress whites. He brought his camera to dinner and asked the waitress to take a few pictures of them. They both ordered the Thanksgiving dinner, complete with turkey, stuffing, mashed potatoes, and, of course, cranberry sauce. Dinner was lovely and she had definitely calmed down.

After dinner, they decided to take a walk around the hotel. Liv went into the ladies' room and when she came out, Kurt was holding a bottle of champagne and two glasses.

"I thought we could walk down to the beach," he said. "There's a full moon tonight."

"Sounds great."

On the beach, they walked towards the rock jetty. Kurt extended his hand and helped Liv up onto the rocks where they sat down. Kurt opened the champagne and poured two glasses. The moon was shining down on the ocean. *Gorgeous*, Liv thought.

"Well, Liv, cheers. Happy Thanksgiving."

"Cheers."

"Liv, let me ask you, was this the best Thanksgiving that you've ever had?"

"What?"

"Well, what I mean is, is there anything that I can do to make this the best Thanksgiving of your life?"

Oh my God, she thought, *he wants to have sex on the rocks!*

"Kurt, honestly, it was a perfect Thanksgiving."

Kurt put his champagne glass down. He then stood up and got down on one knee.

"Well, Liv, this would be the best Thanksgiving of *my* life if you would agree to be my wife." He pulled out a small black velvet box from his pocket and opened it. Inside was a two-caret diamond solitaire engagement ring.

She grabbed the ring and held it up to the moon. "Kurt is this your idea of a joke? Where did you get this, out of a Cracker Jack box? Kurt, you have a very sick sense of humor."

"Liv, please be careful with that. That's two months of my salary that you're holding. Liv, please, I'm not joking. If you don't believe me, go call your parents. Your whole family is waiting for us to call. Even your grandparents."

Liv jumped down from the rocks, still holding the ring, and ran up to the payphone at the pool. Kurt followed right behind. Liv dialed her parents' number and her mother answered on the first ring.

"Mom?"

"Liv! Oh my gosh, we're all so excited and happy for you!"

"Mom, you knew about this?"

"Yes! Kurt called us two months ago and asked permission to marry you."

Liv looked over at Kurt and said, "You called my parents?"

Kurt got down on one knee once again. He took the ring from Liv's hand and began to slide it onto her ring finger. "Liv, will you please be my wife?"

"Oh, my gosh, yes! Yes, of course!"

On the other end of the phone, Liv could hear her mother yelling, "She said yes!" She could hear her whole family cheering. Kurt stood up and kissed her. Liv couldn't wait to be Mrs. Kurt Donovan!

CHAPTER 15

MEET THE FAMILY

The next six months were a whirlwind. Kurt and Liv would be married on June 14th at The Breakers Hotel in Palm Beach. Liv's grandparents and parents were married there, so she wanted to keep with the tradition. She was going to be the first of the next generation in her family to be married.

Her family was sparing no expense for her special day. Her dress would be made by Priscilla of Boston (they had also designed Grace Kelly's wedding dress). Liv had decided on an ivory wedding dress that was off the shoulder. Beautiful roses surrounded the cuffed sleeves. The bottom of the dress was satin with lace trim. The lace had small pearls sewn into it and sequins. The back of the dress had over a hundred small satin buttons. Her veil had matching lace trim and a matching rose headpiece. It was a dream of a dress. For flowers, Liv chose white and ivory roses. She also insisted upon having white hydrangeas because they reminded her of the Jersey Shore in the summer.

Kurt and Liv would be married at 4:30 p.m. at the Church of Bethesda-by-the-Sea, with the reception following at The Breakers in the Mediterranean Ballroom. Her family even decided to rent old-fashioned trolleys for the weekend to shuttle guests around the island of Palm Beach.

Everything was going according to plan until Christmas. Liv and Kurt decided to spend Christmas in New Jersey with her parents. Their engagement announcement was in the *Asbury Park Press* and the *Palm Beach Post*. Her parents even threw them an engagement party at the Manasquan River Country Club. It was a joyous time for the Gallagher family. They embraced Kurt with open arms, and the joy they got every time Liv looked at Kurt was priceless. These two were definitely in love.

Two days after Christmas, they flew to Asheville, North Carolina, to spend one night with Kurt's family before Kurt would have to return to California. Kurt's grandparents, Fred and Mary, lived in a small three-bedroom, log cabin home complete with a woodburning stove and fireplace. The home was located at the foot of the Great Smoky Mountains.

When they arrived, Mary had prepared tea for everyone, setting out her best tea set on a lace tablecloth. She had cookies fresh out of the oven. Liv was touched that Mary had obviously gone out of her way to impress her and make her feel welcome. They all sat down in front of the fireplace to catch up.

"I'm so happy I finally get to see where Kurt grew up," Liv smiled.

"Well, it's not much, but it's home," Fred said.

"The drive here was beautiful," Liv continued. "The mountains and trees are covered with snow. It looks like an enchanted forest."

"Kurt, did you drive her in through town?" asked Fred.

"Yes, sir," Kurt answered. "I showed her the main street, my high school, and where Mom lives."

"Well, we'll see your mom tonight at Pack's," Fred said. "We're supposed to meet her for dinner after she gets off work at the bank."

Kurt turned to Liv. "Pack's Tavern. I've been going there my whole life. I think you'll like it."

"Sounds good," Liv said

"Well…I want to hear all about the wedding plans," Mary smiled.

Liv began to fill them in.

"Well, just so you know," Fred interjected, "we've booked a room at the Colony Hotel. The Breakers was a little too pricey for us."

"I meant to tell you, my cousin actually has a guest house very close to The Breakers and has invited all of you to stay there," said Liv. "We thought you might be more comfortable."

"That's real nice," said Fred. "I think we'll take you up on that. But we'd like to pitch in for the rehearsal dinner, if that's okay."

"Of course," Liv said.

"Where is it being held?" Mary asked.

"At Al Fresco," replied Liv. "It's a very casual restaurant on the beach. The food is amazing and the views of the ocean and golf course are very pretty."

"Sounds lovely, dear. And where is the wedding ceremony?"

"Grammy, I told you," said Kurt, "it's at the Church of Bethesda-by-the-Sea."

"Is that a Catholic church, Kurt?"

"No, Grammy, it's an Episcopal church."

"But…but Kurt, we're Catholic," said Mary, suddenly frowning. "They'll still have communion at least, right?"

"Well, no, Grammy. The service is only forty-five minutes long. There won't be time."

"I see," said Mary, rising from her chair. "Well. I think I'll go lie down before dinner. Please help yourself to more tea and cookies."

Kurt and Liv looked at each other as Mary left the room.

Fred leaned towards them and said, "Don't worry, she'll be fine. Listen, let me help you with your things. We've made up the loft—Kurt's old bedroom—for the two of you for tonight. It might be a little chilly up there, but I suppose you two can keep each other warm, right?"

Liv blushed slightly, surprised that Kurt's grandparents were allowing them to sleep together. That would certainly never happen at her family's home.

After Kurt and Liv got settled in, they went back downstairs and before long, everyone was piling into Fred's old Buick station wagon for the drive to Pack's Tavern, a casual pub with heavy wood and soft lighting. Fred and Mary waved to some of the other customers and Liv could tell that this was the kind of small-town establishment where the locals liked to gather.

When they arrived, Kurt's mother Lisa was seated at a corner booth enjoying a cocktail. Everyone greeted each other and they all squeezed into the booth. The waitress came and took their drink orders. Lisa downed her remaining Scotch and asked for another one.

"Well, Liv," said Lisa, "tell me all about the wedding. Do you have a dress?"

"Oh, yes, and I'm very excited about it. I'm getting it made from Priscilla of Boston."

The waitress returned with their drinks. Lisa took a big sip of her Scotch and started choking. Then she took out a pack of Marlboro Lights, lit one, and took a long drag. "Liv, this dress of yours...how much does it cost?"

"Mother, please," Kurt said.

"I'm just asking, Kurt. I'm guessing it's more than I make in a year at the bank."

Liv looked around nervously.

"Mom, please don't do this," said Kurt.

"Do what? Kurt, are you sure you want to marry this princess? We're hardworking, simple people, you know!"

Liv jumped in. "Ms. Donovan, I can assure you I'm not a princess. My family has worked very hard their entire lives. They're all just very excited about the wedding."

Lisa rolled her eyes. "Kurt, if you want to marry this princess, that's your choice, but I think you're making a big mistake."

"Mom, please," said Kurt, looking at his grandparents for help, but neither were looking up from their menus.

"Now if you'll excuse me, I really must be going." Lisa left the table and marched out of the restaurant.

"Sorry about that, Liv," Kurt said. "She's really a nice person. It's just that, well, when she gets to drinking, she can be a little… difficult. Don't take anything she said seriously."

Liv was speechless. She had never been treated like this in her entire life. This was going to be her mother-in-law?

When the waitress arrived back to the table with their dinners, they all sat more or less in silence as they ate.

Finally, Kurt said, "Grappy, don't you have anything to say?"

"Son, when you've been married as long as we have, there isn't much else to talk about. She's heard all of my stories and I've heard all of hers. Just wait, you'll see." Kurt and Liv looked at each other.

When they arrived back at Fred and Mary's house, Liv and Kurt said goodnight and retreated to the loft. Liv was freezing even though she was wearing the silk long underwear that Kurt had given her for Christmas. She crawled into bed next to Kurt hoping to get warm.

"Kurt?" she said.

"Yes?"

"Your family hates me."

"Now, don't say that. They don't even know you."

"Well, your mother certainly hates me."

"I told you not to take her seriously. Not when she's drinking."

"And your grandparents are sweet, but why didn't you tell me that this Catholic thing was such a big deal to them? You never even mentioned it."

"I never mentioned it because it doesn't matter to me. I just want to marry you. I love you."

"I love you, too."

"Now, try to get some sleep. We both have early flights tomorrow."

Liv closed her eyes, but it was clear that she and Kurt really did come from two different worlds. And Kurt was right. His family really didn't know her and she really didn't know them. Maybe she was rushing into this marriage. Or was it just cold feet?

CHAPTER 16

A FORK IN THE ROAD

Liv looked out her classroom window and saw the light snow beginning to fall. She was back in Annapolis and Kurt had returned to the naval base on Coronado. He had successfully made it through Hell Week. Seventy-five percent of his class had dropped out, but not Kurt. He was now officially a Navy SEAL. He was waiting to find out if he was going to be stationed at Coronado or Little Creek, Virginia. Liv had notified St. Mary's that she would not be returning in the fall. She was looking forward to living and teaching on the naval base in Coronado or Virginia. She really didn't have a preference for where she lived. She was just looking forward to being Kurt's wife.

Everything was going according to plan until President Clinton announced his plan for a $14 billion cut-back in the military. On Friday, January 14, Kurt and his team were all called in for an emergency meeting. Much to Kurt's surprise, he learned very quickly that President Clinton's plan was being put into action. At the meeting, he and his team were all offered an early retirement package. The package would allow Kurt to leave the military immediately with full military benefits for life. They were all given the weekend to consider the offer. Kurt struggled all weekend with his decision. He thought about calling Liv but he felt that this was a decision that he had to make on his own. The fact is, he had experienced base life firsthand by now. The husbands were deployed for months at a time; the wives were left alone. There was a high rate of infidelity and divorce.

By Monday, Kurt's decision was clear. He decided if he really wanted his marriage to work, he needed to leave the military and that's exactly what he did. He signed the release papers, packed up his truck, and headed back to Annapolis.

On Thursday afternoon, Liv arrived home to find Kurt's truck parked in front of her townhouse. *What on earth?* she thought.

She went inside to find Kurt sitting on the couch.

"Kurt, is everything okay? What are you doing here?" Kurt told Liv everything. She had very mixed feelings. She had made peace with living on the base and being a military wife. To make matters worse, their wedding was just a few months away. "Kurt, what do you plan to do now?"

"Well, Liv, the only life I've ever known is the military, but I need to find a job and fast. I can't marry you being unemployed."

"Well, why don't you work for the family's business? I know they would hire you. Plus, every man in my family works there. It's who we are."

Kurt took Liv's hands.

"Liv, that's a great offer but I really want us to find our own way. I want us to be partners and build a life together. It's also very important for me to be a self-made man. No one has ever had to give me anything and I want to keep it that way. Just trust me, okay?"

"Okay."

"Liv, don't worry. It will all work out. Please have faith."

In less than two weeks, Kurt had secured a job with Lanier Worldwide, based out of Owings Mills, Maryland. Basically, he was selling copy machines out of his truck. He told Liv this was a temporary job, but the fact that he was in sales would look good on his résumé.

To say that Liv's parents were upset would be a huge understatement. They respected the fact that Kurt wanted to make his own way in the world but they were worried about their daughter. Since Liv had given notice at her current teaching job, St. Mary's had already hired a new teacher for the following year. She had also not renewed the lease on her townhouse because she thought she would be living on the naval base with Kurt, and the owners wanted her out by June 1st. Somehow, their bright future wasn't looking so bright anymore.

CHAPTER 17

FOR BETTER OR WORSE

May 14th, 1994, one month before the wedding, Kurt and Liv had decided to rent a two-story brick home in Bethesda, Maryland, right off of the East-West Highway. The home had wood floors, a huge backyard, screened in sunporch, a fireplace, and three bedrooms upstairs.

Liv loved the house, but it was her new teaching job that she wasn't very excited about. She needed a job in the fall, so she took a teaching position in Silver Springs, Maryland. The school was on the border of Maryland and Washington, DC. It was basically an inner city school that was located in a rough neighborhood. That part really didn't bother her. What bothered her were the long hours she was going to have to work. Her teaching contract had her working the before and aftercare school programs, 7:00 a.m. to 7:00 p.m. And to make matters worse, her kindergarten classroom was in the basement (no windows and it was right next to the kitchen). Her salary for the year was $19,000 with no health insurance or overtime pay. She decided to take the job because, in the end, the most important thing was that Kurt and she were finally going to be together.

On the weekends, she and Kurt would drive to Bethesda to fix up their new home. They painted the interior, put wallpaper up in the dining room and master bedroom, and even planted a vegetable garden in the backyard. Liv's lease was up on her townhouse on June 1st. So, they would move into their new home two weeks before their wedding.

Liv's grandparents surprised them with a trip to the Capa Juluca Resort in Anguilla for their honeymoon. It was full steam ahead. Liv couldn't wait to be Mrs. Kurt Donovan.

CHAPTER 18

THE REHEARSAL DINNER

One week until Liv and Kurt would say "I do." All of their friends and family had descended on the island of Palm Beach. The week was full of wedding activities. There was a bridesmaid's luncheon at Taboo and a bachelorette spa day at the Ritz. Liv's cousin Bob hosted a golf outing at the Everglades Club for all of the men in the family and the groomsmen. It was a week full of celebrations! The rehearsal dinner was at Al Fresco, a beautiful two-story, yellow historic home with black shutters complete with wraparound balconies. The restaurant was known for its excellent Italian cuisine and beautiful ocean views.

The week was absolutely perfect, except for one thing. Liv couldn't help but notice that at all of the wedding events, Kurt's mother was, well, there's no nice way of saying this—simply drinking way too much. And the things that were coming out of her mouth were outrageous! Liv's mom was very concerned and found her behavior to be completely inappropriate.

After the rehearsal dinner, Kurt pulled Liv's parents aside for a private conversation.

"I would first like to thank both of you for this incredible week and for welcoming me into your family," he said. "Also, I really want to apologize for my mother's behavior. I think she's been extremely nervous about the wedding, and she's definitely out of her element. My family has rarely traveled outside of Asheville. But I want you to know that I promise to treat your daughter like gold. I know you're worried about my current job situation, and rightfully so, but I'm a hard worker and I'm going to provide Liv with a luxurious lifestyle. She is, and will always be, my princess. She will never want for anything. I can promise you that. I plan to give her a huge home with servants. And anything her heart desires. Your daughter is my everything."

"Kurt," Liv's mom interrupted, "I appreciate what you're saying, but we know our daughter. She doesn't need a mansion with servants. That will never make her happy. All she has ever wanted is a man who loves her, children, and a charming home with a white picket fence. If you can give her those things, she will be happy forever. Now, please go back to the hotel and get a good night's sleep. It's a big day tomorrow. And stop worrying. The wedding is going to be perfect. Oh, and by the way, you're riding in the limo with me tomorrow. So I'll come by your room around 3:30."

"Okay," Kurt nodded. "And thanks again for everything."

Liv's dad reached out and shook Kurt's hand. "Son, it's our pleasure. And welcome to the family."

CHAPTER 19

OUR WEDDING DAY

The morning of June 14, 1994, Liv rolled over and opened her eyes in the Imperial Suite of The Breakers. The sun was shining through the plantation shutters and her wedding dress was hanging in the window. Her wedding day had finally arrived. Soon, there was a bustle of activity outside of her bedroom door. Her mother had arranged for a breakfast buffet in the suite's dining room for Liv and her bridesmaids. The makeup and hair team was setting up in the bathroom. Nothing was being left to chance. This day had to be perfect.

Liv decided to go down to the fitness center to get away from the chaos. She jumped on the treadmill and ran three and a half miles. She then went into the ladies' locker room and threw on her bathing suit. She walked down to the beach and dove into the ocean. The water felt amazing. As she floated on her back in the sea and stared up at the sky, she could hardly believe that within a few hours she was going to be Mrs. Kurt Donovan.

When she returned to the suite, her mother asked, "Liv, where have you been?"

"I went to work out and then I went down to the beach for a quick swim."

"Well, I'm glad you're back. Now, you really need to eat something. We can't have you fainting on the altar!"

"Okay, Mom. Okay."

As Liv went to fix herself a plate, there was a knock at the door. Her mother answered and then turned back toward her daughter.

"Liv, there's a gentleman here to see you."

Liv went to the door.

"Are you Olivia Whittaker?" the man said.

"Yes," replied Liv.

"Soon-to-be Mrs. Donovan?"

"Yes," Liv said, smiling.

"Well, Mr. Donovan asked me to deliver this." From his pocket, the man pulled out a small blue Tiffany's box that was tied in a white satin ribbon. He handed it to her along with a small gift card.

"Liv, read the card," her sister said.

Liv opened the gift card and read it out loud: "*Dear Liv, I want us both to remember this day always. You are my whole world. I love you today and always. Kurt xoxoxo.*"

Then Liv opened the box. Inside was an aquamarine ring surrounded by diamonds. "Oh my gosh! It's beautiful!" Liv said.

Her bridesmaids gathered around to see the ring.

"Let me see it!" Leslie said.

"Wow, he sure has great taste," Katherine said.

"Put it on!" Sarah said.

"Liv, the ring is absolutely exquisite," her mom said, "but we are starting to run behind schedule. Girls, you all need to go back to your rooms to get changed. And please remember to be in the lobby by 3:00 sharp. The limos will be waiting to take you over to the church."

Liv said goodbye to her bridesmaids and then went into the bathroom to jump into the shower. She then sat down to meet with the hair and makeup team. Two hours later, she was ready to put on her wedding dress. Her mother and aunt held the wedding dress as Liv carefully stepped into it. They then lifted the dress and slowly began to button all 100 buttons that ran down the back of the dress.

Liv's mom pinned the veil on her head and handed her the bouquet. Dovey had given her a new strand of pearls—something new. Her aunt had given her a handkerchief—something borrowed. Finally, Liv was wearing a blue garter belt—something blue.

Liv turned around and faced the mirror. Her mother's eyes filled with tears. This was the moment she had been waiting for since Liv was a little girl. "Are you ready to get married, Liv?" she said.

"Yes, Mom. I'm ready."

Then her mother wiped away her tears and said, "Okay, well then I'm going to head over to Kurt's room. I'll see you at the church, darling. Your father is on his way up. And your Rolls Royce is out front. Well, I guess that's everything."

"Thanks, Mom," said Liv. "I love you."

"I love you, too. And just look at you. You're stunning, Liv. Absolutely stunning." They hugged and Liv's mom turned and left the suite.

When Kurt opened the door to his room, he was half dressed. He was still in his boxers, his shirt was unbuttoned, and he was holding his bowtie.

"Kurt, what's going on? You should be dressed by now!"

"I know, but I can't figure out how to tie this thing. Not to mention that these cuff links and button covers are impossible!"

"Okay, no worries. Here, let me help you." Liv's mom went into action and in no time the both of them were in the limo and heading over to the church.

Up in Liv's suite, her father knocked on the door and entered.

"Wow," he beamed. "You look like an angel."

"Thanks, Daddy. You look pretty good yourself."

"Are you ready to go?"

"I'm ready," she said nodding.

When they got in the back of the Rolls Royce, Liv's dad reached over and grabbed her hand. "Liv, are you sure about this? I'm just saying that if you're not sure, we could go over to Tessa's and get a slice of strawberry pie."

"I'm sure, Daddy," she giggled.

"Well, okay then. Driver, take us to the church. My daughter's getting married today!"

When they arrived, Liv and her father were escorted into a side room in the front of the church. There they waited until they heard the orchestra begin to play Pachelbel's Canon in D. The church looked magnificent! Up at the altar, huge candelabras were lit. The altar and pews were draped in flowers—roses, peonies, and hydrangeas. At the end of each pew were candles surrounded by flowers. The church had taken on a magical, romantic glow.

Liv looked at Kurt standing up at the altar. He looked so very handsome, and she noticed that his eyes were full of tears. As she walked towards him, she realized she wasn't nervous at all. This was the man. This was her husband.

She and her father walked slowly together along the red carpet. When they reached the altar, her father lifted her veil and kissed her on the cheek.

The minister asked, "Who gives this woman to be wed?"

"Her mother and I do," said Liv's father. Then he turned and took his seat. The ceremony continued with a reading of Corinthians 13 and Liv's favorite hymn, "I Sing a Song of the Saints of God." The minister began his sermon, speaking about what marriage is and should be. He made note of the fact that as he had gotten to know Liv and Kurt, he'd noticed that they were always holding hands. "God has brought them together," he said. "And may no man tear them apart."

Then it was time for the exchanging of the rings. "Do you, Liv, take Kurt to be your husband?"

"I do." Kurt slipped a diamond wedding band on Liv's finger.

"And do you, Kurt, take Liv to be your wife?" continued the minister.

"I do." Liv slipped Kurt's gold wedding band on his finger.

"By the power vested in me by the state of Florida, I now pronounce you husband and wife. Kurt, you may kiss your bride."

Kurt leaned Liv over and kissed her. The whole church stood up and cheered.

As they ran out of the church doors, a sea of rice followed them. They jumped into the back of the Rolls Royce!

Kurt gazed into Liv's eyes. "You're finally my wife. Kiss me!!"

Liv leaned over and kissed Kurt.

And with that, they were off to the reception.

CHAPTER 20

IT HAD TO BE YOU

When Liv and Kurt pulled up to The Breakers, their wedding planner, the concierge, and a few other staff members from the hotel were outside waiting to greet them. Lisa, the wedding planner, pulled the newlyweds aside.

"Welcome back, Mr. and Mrs. Donovan. If you would please follow me, I would love to show you the ballroom before the wedding guests arrive."

"We can't wait," said Liv.

When they entered the Mediterranean Ballroom, Liv could hardly believe her eyes. Candlelight filled the room. Ivory beeswax candles covered by hurricane glass were on every table. The centerpieces were the same flowers as the church—ivory roses, pink peonies, and white hydrangeas. In the center of the room was the wedding cake—a five-tier, buttercream, basketweave cake accented by real white roses. The cake filling was mascarpone whipped cream with fresh strawberries. It was a romantic dream come true.

Best of all, Liv's grandfather had flown in Harry Connick Jr.

and his seventeen-piece band to play at the reception. The reception was beyond Kurt and Liv's wildest dreams.

"I hope we've met all of your expectations," said Lisa.

"You definitely have," Kurt said.

"It's perfect," replied Liv.

"Fantastic! We're so glad that you're both so pleased. The wedding photographer is waiting down on the beach for you and the wedding party."

"Great," Kurt said. "And thank you again for everything."

The sun was beginning to set. Liv and Kurt strolled along the beach holding hands. Then Kurt picked Liv up and kissed her. The photographer followed along capturing every magical moment. Liv felt as if she was floating on air.

As the cocktail hour wound down, the guests slowly began to enter the ballroom. The guest were greeted by men in tuxedos serving glasses of Veuve Clicquot on silver trays. The wedding party, Kurt, and Liv lined up outside of the ballroom waiting to be announced. The double doors opened and Harry Connick Jr. began introducing the wedding party.

"Finally," he said, "it gives me great pleasure to introduce to you, for the very first time, Mr. and Mrs. Kurt Donovan!" All of the guests stood and applauded.

Liv and Kurt entered the ballroom holding hands and went straight onto the dance floor for their first dance. Harry and his band began to play "It Had to Be You." Liv and Kurt glided across the dance floor staring lovingly into each other's eyes. When the song ended, they took their seats at the head table. Toasts were made, dinner was served, and the guests clinked their champagne glasses for Liv and Kurt to kiss.

Everything was perfect, except for one thing. Kurt's mother had decided to wear a white dress suit with a matching pillbox hat. With a veil, no less. Liv's mom, grandmother, and aunt were appalled.

"Who does she think she is?" said Liv's grandmother. "The bride?"

"It's a well-known wedding etiquette fact that no one should wear white to a wedding except for the bride. That woman has no class," said Liv's mom.

This was only the third wedding that Liv had ever attended and so she couldn't understand what all the fuss was about. Besides, she didn't want anything to ruin her and Kurt's special day. *If this is the worst thing that she does today,* Liv thought to herself, *we'll all be just fine.*

After all the guests had finished dining on surf and turf, it was time for Liv to dance with her father. As they danced to the song "Wind Beneath My Wings," Liv's father whispered to her, "You know you'll always be my baby girl, no matter what. Right?"

"I know, Daddy, and thank you so very much for this wonderful day!"

As the song ended, Kurt tapped Liv's dad on the shoulder and said, "May I please have this next dance?"

Liv smiled and said, "Of course." The band played "Shameless," the first song she and Kurt had ever danced to on the night that they first met.

Liv looked up at Kurt. "I can't believe I'm finally your wife. I've never been this happy."

Kurt kissed her. "And it's just the beginning, my love."

After hours of dancing, it was finally time to cut the cake. Liv and Kurt slowly cut the cake together. It was a very sweet, romantic moment as they both fed each other a small bite of cake. Then it was time to toss the garter belt and the bouquet. Liv turned around and tossed the bouquet over her shoulder. Much to her family's delight, her cousin Leslie caught it. Leslie hadn't had much luck in the romance department. Her grandmother was always saying, "She's not getting any younger, you know." It was a great way to end the evening.

Kurt and Liv said their goodbyes to their guests and headed up to the honeymoon suite. As they opened the double doors to the Royal Poinciana Suite, Kurt picked Liv up and carried her over the threshold. Kurt followed a trail of red rose petals and candles leading to the four-post bed. Next to the bed was a bottle of champagne on ice. Kurt placed Liv down onto the bed and then took off his tuxedo jacket and began to unbutton his shirt.

Liv leaned over and kissed him. "I'll be right back." She headed into the bathroom to put on an all-white, mesh, see-through nightgown.

When she walked out, Kurt picked her up and laid her down on the bed. "Tonight, I get to make love to my wife." And that he did. In the bed, on the floor, outside on the balcony under the stars, and finally, as the sun began to rise, in the shower. Kurt and Liv didn't sleep at all that night.

At 7:00 a.m., they were in the back of a limo heading down to the Miami International Airport to catch their flight to Anguilla. Liv reached over and grabbed Kurt's hand. She couldn't stop looking at her wedding band. *Wow,* she thought. *What a wild ride this has been so far. And to think it's only just the beginning.*

CHAPTER 21

THE HONEYMOON

After a three-hour and ten-minute flight, Kurt and Liv's plane finally touched down on the island of St. Maarten where they had a thirty-minute layover before their next flight. They felt like they had been traveling forever. Finally, they boarded a ten-passenger prop plane for a ten-minute flight over to the island of Anguilla where their plane touched down on a small, unpaved runway. Kurt and Liv were handed their luggage after stepping off the plane and then made it through customs in the tiny airport in less than fifteen minutes. Walking out of the airport, they saw a staff member from the resort waiting for them.

"Welcome to Anguilla, Mr. and Mrs. Donovan. I am Charles, and I will be taking you over to the resort. Please allow me to take care of your luggage."

"Thank you," Kurt said. "It's been a long travel day."

Charles opened the back door of the Lincoln Navigator for Kurt and Liv, loaded the luggage into the trunk, and then slid into the driver's seat.

"Anguilla is not the easiest place to get to," he said, "but I think, by the end of your trip, you'll see it was worth the long travel day. Please sit back and relax. We are only ten minutes away from Capa Juluca."

"How big is the island?" Kurt asked.

"Only sixteen miles long."

They drove along bumpy, unpaved roads and had to stop frequently to allow chickens, roosters, and goats to cross. Charles beeped and waved at pedestrians and passing cars as they drove through the West Village. Liv noticed right away that it seemed to be a very friendly island. As they came around the bend, Liv caught her first view of the ocean. The water was an amazing color that was a mix of turquoise blue and emerald green. She had been to the Bahamas many times, but this island was completely different.

In the distance, Liv saw the Moorish-style white buildings of the resort, which sat on the beach like large sugar cubes. It was a mix between *Arabian Nights* and over-the-top luxury. Charles drove through the resort's gates and then parked in front of the open-air lobby. "Please wait here. I have to go inside and grab the keys to your villa," he said.

Kurt and Liv were speechless. The resort was glamorous and definitely much more than they both had expected. Fifteen villas lined the two miles of the pristine private beach that was set along the cove of Maundays Bay. The bluest of water rolled up onto the white powdered sand. It was heaven on earth.

Shortly, Charles got back into the car. "You're going to be staying in villa number three, of course, the honeymoon suite."

When they pulled up to their villa, a man was waiting for them with two rum punches in hand. "Hello, and welcome to Capa Juluca. My name is Henry, and I will be your private butler for the week. If you need anything at all, I am here to assist you. Now, if you will please follow me, I will show you around your villa."

Kurt and Liv glanced at each other and smiled in disbelief.

Henry opened the villa's courtyard doors. In the courtyard was their own private infinity pool, which was surrounded by a lush, tropical garden.

They followed Henry up four steps. At the top of the steps was a set of giant sliding glass doors that Henry opened for them. Once inside, they were both captivated by the beauty of the villa. Sheer white curtains danced in the balmy island air. The interior of the villa was all white except for the bouquets of tropical flowers that were placed tastefully around the room. There was a four-post bed, a living room, dining room, huge soaking tub, and, best of all, the entire villa looked out at the ocean.

"Wow," said Kurt, looking at Liv. "Your grandparents did good."

"No," Liv replied, "They did great!"

"I'm glad you both are pleased. I will leave you two to get settled," Henry said. "If you need anything, just press the number two on the phone's keypad. I will be at your service twenty-four hours a day."

"Oh, Henry," said Kurt, "I was hoping we could rent a car so we could explore the island while we're here. Could you help me with that?"

"Of course. If you'll just follow me up to the front desk, we can take care of the rental car paperwork."

"Great." Kurt kissed Liv. "I'll be right back."

"Okay. I think I'll call my mom and let her know that we've arrived safely."

"Okay. Make sure to tell her how amazing this place is."

"Oh, don't worry, I will. I can't wait to talk to her."

Henry and Kurt walked out of the villa and Liv reached for the phone.

"Hi, Mom!" she said after the international operator had put her call through. "Oh, my gosh! We made it! This place is amazing. It's beyond beautiful. I'll never be able to thank Dovey and Poppy enough!"

"I'm glad that you arrived safe and sound, but we need to have a serious talk. Where's Kurt?"

"He went to the front desk to rent us a car. Why?"

"Well, Liv, I have to tell you something."

"Mom, what's wrong?"

"Liv, something happened last night after you left the reception."

"What?"

"Well, around midnight, the hotel informed us that they wanted to shut down the ballroom for the night."

"Okay..."

"Well, a number of guests weren't ready to go to bed, so your father invited them to join us for cigars and after dinner drinks at the outdoor bar."

"Okay, Mom, so why are you so upset? Is it about the bar bill? I know the wedding was very expensive."

"Liv, please just stop talking and listen to what I have to tell you."

"Okay, I'm listening."

"Liv, as we were all walking to the outdoor bar, we passed the jacuzzi. Kurt's mother...Liv, Kurt's mother..."

"Mom, what? Just tell me!"

"Kurt's mother was in the jacuzzi, naked, having sex with Kurt's best man, Paul!"

"*What?!* Oh, my God! Paul's married for God's sakes! I can't believe this is happening! How could she do this!?"

"Liv, the whole wedding party saw them. Everyone knows! It was just awful."

"Mom, what am I going to do? I'm on my honeymoon for God's sakes!"

"Liv, I want you to listen to me. You can't tell Kurt. He'll find out, believe me. But it shouldn't come from you. Have you ever heard of the old saying 'killing the messenger'? Well, this applies very well to this situation. Please take my advice on this one. I've been married for a very long time and I know what I'm talking about."

"I don't know, Mom. I don't think this is a very good way to start out my marriage, by keeping a secret this big from my brand-new husband."

"Liv, you have to trust me on this. Don't say a word."

"Okay, I don't agree with this, but okay."

"Liv, I thought your father was going to kill the both of them with his bare hands. Now, I know this is hard, but please try to enjoy your honeymoon."

"I will, Mom. I mean, we're in this magical place and I'm with the man that I have been dreaming about for my entire life."

"Okay, that's my girl. Now go have fun."

"I will, I promise. Love you, Mom."

"Love you, too."

Liv hung up the phone and stared at the receiver. *Wow! What a mess*, she thought. Just then, Kurt walked into the villa, holding a set of keys.

"I got us a Jeep Wrangler for the week!"

For the rest of the week, Liv decided to take her mother's advice. After all, what was done was done, and you do only have one honeymoon.

Liv and Kurt had a fabulous time exploring the island. They went to dinner in town at Blanchard's Beach Shack, Mangoes, and Koal Keel. The people on the island were very kind and hospitable. The couple spent their days sailing, going to the spa, and sunbathing on the beach. They met another couple, Nancy and Lance from England, who were also on their honeymoon. Nancy was a free spirit, and Lance was a little more uptight, but they were both a lot of fun. Lance was a very successful stockbroker in London. Kurt was very interested in knowing all about his line of work. After all, Kurt didn't want to be selling copiers forever.

For the last night of their honeymoon, the hotel arranged a special farewell dinner at their oceanfront restaurant, Pimms. Liv was in the bathroom getting ready for dinner when she remembered it was time to take her birth control pill. As she held the pill in her hand, she started thinking. Then she walked out of the bathroom holding her pill case.

"Kurt?" she said.

"Yes?"

"I need to talk to you about something."

"Okay."

"Well, you know, I haven't been thrilled with the side effects of these things. And, well, we are married now."

"Liv, what are you trying to say?"

"I don't want to take these anymore."

"Liv, we can't start a family now. Are you crazy?"

"Kurt, I agree, but I really want to stop taking them."

"Well, if they're making you feel that awful, we'll just have to think of something else to use for birth control." He then took the pill case out of Liv's hands and threw it into the waste basket. He leaned over and kissed her. "Now, I would like to make love to my wife before dinner, if that's okay?"

Liv went over to the giant sliding glass doors and opened them, allowing the ocean air to fill the room. She then untied her robe and walked over to the bed. She rolled Kurt over onto his back.

"I love making love to you, Mr. Donovan." And, with that, she climbed on top of him. They never made it to dinner that night.

CHAPTER 22

SECRETS REVEALED

Three weeks after Liv and Kurt had returned from their honeymoon, they were just starting to settle into married life. Thankfully, Kurt still did not know about his mother's indiscretion at the wedding. Liv's new teaching job didn't start until after the Labor Day weekend, so she was enjoying her new roles as a wife and homemaker. She cleaned the house, ran errands, did the laundry, and made sure there was a nice dinner on the table when Kurt got home from work.

After meeting Lance and Nancy on their honeymoon, Kurt had decided that he wanted to become a stockbroker. He knew that selling copiers wasn't going to keep a roof over their heads or provide them with the lifestyle that he so desperately wanted for the both of them. He had set up an initial interview with Goldman Sachs in Rockville. In the meantime, Kurt had put Liv and himself on a strict monthly budget. Liv didn't mind the budget one bit. She was glad that they were working as a team to build their future. Although Liv did have a trust fund, her parents had made it very clear to her that the money in her trust was for emergency use only. It was not to live off of.

Liv came downstairs on Sunday morning dressed and ready to run their weekend errands. She found Kurt on the sunporch drinking coffee and going over a stack of papers.

"Kurt, what are you doing? I thought we were going to run errands together."

"Liv, I have to prepare for the Goldman Sachs interview next week. I really want this job."

"I know you do," said Liv, "so I'll tell you what. I'll just go to the grocery store this morning. And next week, I'll do the rest of the errands. That way I'll be back around noon."

"That's perfect," Kurt said. "I should be finished by then and we can go grab some lunch at the Parkway Deli."

"Sounds like a plan."

"And, Liv, I really need you to stick to our weekly budget at the grocery store, and please only use the Discover card."

"Kurt, you worry too much. You tell me the same thing every time I go to the store. But do you want to know something?"

"What?"

"You're very sexy when you're being so serious." She walked over and kissed him goodbye. He slapped her on the backside and with that she was out the door.

At the grocery store, Liv always looked for sale items. Their diet was mainly pot roast, cheeseburgers, meatloaf, spaghetti, macaroni and cheese, hot dogs, and, if they were on sale, Perdue "Oven Stuffer" roasters. Their new budget made them both very grateful for their vegetable garden. In their garden, they were growing lettuce, corn, tomatoes, cucumbers, zucchini, beets, and yellow squash. They ate at home almost every night, but on Friday nights, they'd go out somewhere inexpensive for dinner. Liv made it her mission to try to produce the nicest dinners possible on their tight budget.

After her cart was full, Liv checked out and headed home. When she opened the front door of their home, she stared in disbelief at the scene that was before her. The coffee table was flipped over and the crystal bowl that was on it was smashed. The picture that was hanging over the fireplace was on the floor and glass covered the hardwood. She went through the dining room and into the kitchen. On the kitchen floor was every plate and piece of glassware that they had owned, broken and shattered. Thankfully, their wedding gifts were still at her parents' house.

She knew in that instant that Kurt must have found out about his mother's escapades in the jacuzzi the night of their wedding. She put the groceries on the counter and ran upstairs. Kurt was pacing back and forth in their bedroom. The glass lamp on the nightstand that was filled with seashells was in pieces on the floor.

"Grappy, Liv just walked in. I have to go." With that, he hung up the phone. "Liv, we need to talk. It's about my mother."

Oh, God, she thought, *here it comes.* "Kurt," she interrupted, "I already know all about your mother."

"What do you mean?"

"When I called my mom on our honeymoon, she told me everything."

"What?! Are you kidding me? And you didn't tell me?!"

"Please don't be mad. She told me not to tell you. She told me that you should hear about your mother from someone else and that it shouldn't come from your wife. I can understand if you're upset with me. I honestly just didn't know what to do."

Kurt sat down on the bed. "Well, I sure did hear about everything, all right. Matt called me. [He was a groomsman in their wedding.] He assumed I already knew what had happened and he called to say how sorry he was and to make sure that I was okay. After we hung up, well, I guess I went a little crazy. I'm sorry, Liv.

I'm just in shock, I guess. I know I shouldn't be. She's done stuff like this my whole life. I mean, you've seen how she drinks and behaves. It's embarrassing. I just can't believe this happened the night of our wedding."

Kurt seemed completely deflated and despondent in a way Liv had never seen him before. She felt suddenly overwhelmed with sympathy and compassion for the man she loved. She sat down beside him and put her hand on his thigh as he continued. "Anyway, I called Grappy. I told him I'm through with her. Liv, my grandparents raised me. *They're* the ones who truly matter in my life. My mother has done nothing but disappoint me over and over again and I just can't take it anymore. I want nothing to do with her. We're never going to see her again, and she will never get to know her own grandchildren."

"Are you sure that's what you want?"

Kurt nodded. "Absolutely. And you know what's the worst part, Liv? She ruined our wedding."

"No she didn't. Don't say that. Our wedding was a dream. Please don't let your mother's actions take away our memories of that special day."

"You're right, Liv." Liv kissed Kurt's hand and put her head on his shoulder. "You're my family, Liv," Kurt said. "Now and forever."

CHAPTER 23

THANKSGIVING

5:00 a.m., Thanksgiving morning, Liv was in the kitchen stuffing the Thanksgiving turkey. Her family was coming down from Jersey for Thanksgiving dinner and to see Liv and Kurt's home for the first time. Liv was both nervous and excited to see her family.

It was hard to believe that one year ago today, Kurt had proposed. So much had happened since then—their move, their wedding, and new jobs for both of them.

The dining room table was set with a new Thanksgiving tablecloth, their wedding Wedgwood bone china with emerald green and gold-trim dinner plates, Lenox flatware, Waterford gold-trim crystal wine and champagne goblets, and last but not least, the Spode turkey platter that had been passed down in her family for generations. In the center of the table was a flower arrangement of white and orange roses in a pumpkin vase. Liv thought the table looked perfect.

For dinner, she was cooking all of her family's favorites: turkey with fresh herbs placed under the skin, cornbread stuffing, mashed potatoes, sweet potatoes, green bean casserole, turnips, and creamed spinach. Her mother, thankfully, was bringing the buttermilk biscuits, an apple pie, and a pumpkin pie that she had picked up at the Delicious Orchards in Colts Neck.

Liv was ready to host her first Thanksgiving dinner.

At 9:00 a.m., the doorbell rang. There was Liv's father, mother, sister, Aunt Betty, Uncle Bert, and her grandparents, Dovey and Poppy.

"Come in!"

Kurt and Liv hugged and greeted everyone. After giving them a quick tour of the house, they all gathered in the living room.

"Liv, the house is precious," said Dovey. "It really is. You and Kurt have done a wonderful job."

"Thanks," Liv said, "it's definitely starting to feel like home."

"So what time is dinner?" Liv's dad asked.

"I'm aiming for three o'clock."

"I thought I would take all of you on a short tour of Bethesda, and then we could head down to DC for a bit," said Kurt.

"I'll stay here and help Liv," her sister, Sarah, said.

"Well, I don't mind staying to help, too," said her mom. "Besides, Liv, you look a little pale. Are you feeling okay?"

"Mom, I'm fine. Go sightseeing. This year, you don't have to lift a finger in the kitchen. I've got this."

"Well, in that case, I'll grab my coat."

They all piled into her father's car and were off.

Sarah and Liv headed into the kitchen.

"So how is everything?" Sarah asked.

"It's good, except I really miss teaching at St. Mary's."

"Mom told me about you getting robbed in the school's parking lot."

"Unbelievable. The guy followed me to my car, pulled out a gun, took my wallet, and then ripped the cross necklace off my neck. It was horrible. And I had just cashed my birthday check from Dovey."

"Well, at least Kurt got that job at Goldman Sachs."

"Thank God. The hours are very long," Liv said. "9:00 a.m. to 9:00 p.m. But, at least in a month, we'll both be covered under their health insurance plan."

"Speaking of health, Mom's right, Liv. You do look pale. Are you feeling okay?"

"Yeah. I'm just tired."

Liv went to grab the butter from out of the fridge and glanced at her kitchen calendar. "Sarah?"

"What?"

"I just realized something. I haven't gotten my period this month. I always keep track on the calendar."

"Are you sure?" said Sarah.

"Yes, I'm like a clock. I'm never late."

Sarah ran into the living room and grabbed her coat. "Liv, where's the closest drugstore?" she asked.

"Why?"

"I'm going to buy you a pregnancy test."

"What?"

"You're late, aren't you? So let's find out why."

"I guess you're right. Well, there's the Chevy Chase Pharmacy. It's right up the road."

"Okay. I'll be right back. We need to find out if there's more than one turkey in the oven!"

"Oh, brother!"

In less than fifteen minutes, Sarah was back at the house. "Okay," she said to Liv, "now go upstairs to the bathroom and pee."

"Don't you think we should read the directions first?"

"It's not rocket science. Just pee on the stick."

"Okay, okay, I'm going."

Liv went into the bathroom.

She and her sister stared at the test on the sink's vanity.

"Oh, my gosh, Liv," said Sarah, "there are two lines!"

"No way! Let me see that. You're right!"

"Liv, two lines means you're pregnant!"

"Oh, my gosh! How did this happen?"

"Well, I think we both know how this happened. Oh, wow, Mom and Dad are going to kill you! You're living paycheck to paycheck. You don't even have medical or auto insurance. You're screwed."

"Sarah, stop it! Look, don't say anything. First of all, I need to tell Kurt. Second of all, we're not saying anything today! Besides, these things are wrong all the time."

"On the box it says over ninety-nine percent accurate."

"All right, that's enough. Let's get back in the kitchen. We need to get this dinner on the table by 3:00."

By two o'clock, everyone had arrived back at the house.

"Kurt, can you come upstairs with me for a minute?" said Liv.

Kurt followed Liv upstairs. "Is everything okay?" he said. "How's the dinner coming along? I must say it smells great in here, and I'm starving."

Liv took Kurt's hand and pulled him into the bathroom.

"Liv, what's going on?"

Liv pointed to the pregnancy test on the sink. Kurt picked it up.

"Liv, you're…pregnant?! How did this happen?"

"Kurt, we both know exactly how this happened!"

"What are we going to do?"

"Don't panic. I'm going to go to the clinic tomorrow to make sure. There's no need to say anything to the family until we're 100 percent sure. Okay?"

"Okay," said Kurt, then he hugged and kissed Liv. "Liv, we're going to have a baby. I can hardly believe this. I love you."

"I love you, too."

Kurt placed his hand on Liv's stomach.

Then there was a knock on the bathroom door.

"Is everything all right in there?"

"Everything's fine, Dad."

They opened the door and went downstairs. Neither one could stop smiling.

Everyone gathered around the dining room table.

Liv's grandfather said, "If everyone would please join hands." They all joined hands and bowed their heads. "Dear Lord, I would like to thank you for allowing us to all be together to enjoy this splendid meal. Please bless Kurt and Liv in their new home. Bless our family today and forever. Amen."

"Amen," everybody said.

"Liv, the table is absolutely flawless," her mom said.

"Forget the table," her father said. "The food is fantastic. Liv, you have really outdone yourself!"

Kurt stood up and raised his champagne glass. "I would like to make a toast to my beautiful wife. Thank you for this beautiful meal. Thank you for making a house a home, and thank you for making me the happiest man on earth. Happy Thanksgiving!"

Liv smiled and thought to herself, *This is one Thanksgiving that I will remember always. We're going to have a baby!*

CHAPTER 24

WE'RE HAVING A BABY!

Nine months later—July 1995. Well, apparently those pregnancy tests really were ninety-nine percent accurate. Liv was having a baby! A baby boy, as a matter of fact, that was due on July 23rd. She and Kurt were over the moon, but it hadn't been easy, to say the least. First off, Liv's pregnancy had been very difficult. She had been put on bedrest since April.

Also, she and Kurt had moved. Liv didn't want to raise their baby boy in the city. She wanted more of a country setting, so in March, they had purchased their first home. They were able to get a VA loan because of Kurt's military service and Liv did use her trust fund for the down payment (with her family's blessing, of course). The home was in Barnesville, Maryland, on Peachtree Road. It was a brand new, three-story townhouse with two gas fireplaces, four bedrooms, three and a half baths, a large fenced-in backyard, and a huge deck that overlooked the Bucklodge Conservation Park. Liv and Kurt were in heaven.

Kurt's career at Goldman Sachs had really taken off. He had acquired some high-powered clients from the Washington, DC area. Life was good, but it all came with a price. Liv had been forced to quit her job because she was put on bedrest and she was alone a lot. Kurt was still working from 9:00 a.m. to 9:00 p.m. Liv would joke, "Kurt, you only ever see me in my pajamas."

Thankfully, they lived next to a very nice couple who were in their late sixties—Archie and Jane Collins. They were lifesavers, always there with a casserole in hand, a chat on the deck, or one of Jane's famous pineapple upside-down cakes. Liv missed her family desperately, so she was very grateful to have Archie and Jane next door.

Liv thought she would lose her mind on bedrest. And to make matters even worse, the outdoor thermometer on their deck read 120 degrees. It was a record-breaking heatwave that summer. Liv's OBGYN didn't want her out in the heat, so she spent her days reading, needlepointing a blanket for the baby, and playing solitaire. Also, to pass the time, she decided to write a cookbook that was a compilation of all of her family's favorite recipes. On the weekends, Kurt would go out and put the AC on in the car for at least fifteen minutes, and then they'd go to the movies or to the mall. Liv was definitely ready to have this baby!

Liv's mom arrived at their home on July 21st. Liv was so happy and relieved that her mother was there. She had been to the doctor's that morning and she was only two centimeters dilated. So for the next week, Liv did everything she had ever heard of to go into labor. She ate spicy food. She got a foot massage. She and Kurt drove down bumpy country roads. Her father told her to vacuum. And, finally, she was having a lot of sex with Kurt. (Her doctor's recommendation.)

On July 27th, she was back at the doctor's. Still no progress. Her doctor looked at Kurt and Liv and said, "Well, he just doesn't seem to want to come out. Be at the hospital this afternoon by three o'clock. Liv, by tomorrow, you'll be holding your baby."

Liv and Kurt raced home to tell Liv's mom the news. "Mom, the doctor has decided to induce me this afternoon so we need to get over to the hospital right away. Kurt, do we have everything?"

"Don't worry, I have your suitcase right here," said Kurt. "Liv, we really do need to leave as soon as possible because you know how bad the traffic can get on 270."

"Okay. Mom, let's go," said Liv.

"Wait a minute, Liv," her mother said. "I've been thinking. This is a very special time for you and Kurt. You two should experience the birth of your son alone. I really don't need to be there."

"Mom, are you sure you don't want to come with us?"

"Liv, I'm sure. Besides, who will take care of Buddy? Kurt, just give me a call when the baby is born and I'll come right over."

"I promise to call you the very second that he's born," said Kurt.

"Well, Mom, I guess this is it. I love you."

"I love you, too. I can't believe my baby is having a baby!" said Liv's mom.

And with that, Liv and Kurt were off to the hospital.

CHAPTER 25

A LABOR OF LOVE

By 4:00 p.m., Liv was all checked into her birthing suite at Shady Grove Hospital. She had decided to wait as long as possible to get the epidural. The doctor had started her on an IV drip of Pitocin to speed up her contractions. Finally, at six centimeters, the contractions really started to kick in. The pain was so bad that Liv thought that her body would split in half. She finally asked for the epidural. She turned to Kurt and said, "Kurt, can you please call my mom? I really want her here." Kurt picked up the phone and handed Liv the receiver.

"Mom?" Liv said

"Honey, is everything okay?"

"Mom, I'm scared. I don't think I can do this. I really want you to come over."

"Okay. Just try to stay calm. Women have babies every day."

"I know, Mom, but I had no idea that it was going to be this bad."

"Hang in there. I'll ask Archie and Jane to take care of Buddy. I'll be there as soon as I can."

"Okay, Mom. Just please hurry."

Liv handed the phone back to Kurt. He began rubbing her back.

The anesthesiologist finally arrived. He wheeled in a metal tray table. On it was a very large needle.

"Okay, Liv," the anesthesiologist said, "are you ready for some relief?"

"Yes! Please!"

"Okay, I need you to come over here and sit on the edge of the bed. Kurt, I need you to hold her shoulders. Olivia, it's very important that you don't move. I need you to curve your spine like the letter C. That looks perfect. Now, just don't move. One quick stick, and then we're done."

Liv closed her eyes and tried to stay as still as possible. She felt the needle go in and then she heard a crash. She opened her eyes to see Kurt lying on the floor.

"Oh, boy," said the anesthesiologist. He turned to the nurse. "Go get him some smelling salts, juice, and cookies. Olivia, don't worry. He'll be fine. Just stay still. I'm almost finished."

Three nurses came in to tend to Kurt while the anesthesiologist helped Liv get comfortable back in bed. "Are you feeling a little relief?"

"Oh, yes! Thank you."

Just then, Liv's mom walked into the room.

"What on earth?" she said. "Liv, why is Kurt on the floor?"

"He fainted when he saw the needle for the epidural," said one of the nurses.

"For God's sakes, Kurt, you were a Navy SEAL!"

"I know, Mom," Kurt said, "but that needle was huge."

"Well, let's get you into a chair so you can finish your apple juice and cookies," the nurse said.

Liv's mom rolled her eyes and went over to her daughter. She took Liv's hands. "Are you okay?"

"This is much harder than I thought, Mom. Why don't they show you this in high school in sex ed? No one would ever have sex again!"

Liv's mom laughed. "Don't worry. It's all going to be worth it when you're holding that little baby boy in your arms. By the way, are you two still arguing over his name?"

"We sure are," said Kurt. "I want his name to be Christopher."

"I told you a million times I'm not naming our son Christopher," said Liv.

"Well, you two better think of a name and fast," said Liv's mom.

At 6:00 p.m., Liv's doctor walked into the room to check on her. "Everything looks good," he said. "I have three other patients in labor tonight, so I'll be back to check on you in a little while."

At 8:00 p.m., he returned. "Well, this is going incredibly slowly. I'm going to turn up the Pitocin."

Liv dozed off and on throughout the night. At 11:00 p.m., she rolled over and saw Kurt and her doctor eating pizza and watching the Late Show. *Jeez*, she thought. *They're having a pizza party and I'm over here trying to have a baby.* At midnight the pain was back and worse than ever. "What's going on?" she said.

"We have to let the epidural wear off so you can push," said the doctor. The next hour was pure agony for Liv. Finally, at 1:00 a.m., the doctor said, "Liv, it's time to push." Three pushes later, at 1:15, the doctor said, "Kurt, come here and cut the umbilical cord."

"Oh my gosh. He's out?" Liv said.

"He's out," said the doctor.

"Why isn't he crying?"

The doctor turned the baby over and slapped him on his back three times, then there was a cry. "He was still sleeping," said the doctor, laughing. The nurse lay the baby on Liv's chest.

"Wow," she said. "He's so small."

"Six pounds, eight ounces," the nurse said.

Liv noticed his light brown hair with blond streaks and his beautiful, blue eyes as he looked up at her. "He's so sweet," she said. The baby reached out and grabbed her finger and she kissed him on his hand. "Welcome to the world, my son."

She looked up to see her mom and Kurt holding each other, both of them in tears. "He's perfect, Liv. He's absolutely perfect," said her mom. "And he even has your hair."

Kurt walked over and put his arm around Liv and the baby.

"Would you like to hold your son?" Liv asked. Kurt nodded and she carefully handed him the baby. Kurt looked down at the baby and said, "I love you, son." Then he looked back up at Liv. "Liv, what would you like to name our son?"

Liv answered right away. "His name should be William Peter Gallagher, after my grandfather and father."

"William it is," said Kurt, kissing his son.

"Well, I think that's the perfect choice," said Liv's mom.

Liv thought how bright her future looked. She finally had the family that she had always dreamt of.

CHAPTER 26

SITTING ON A RAINBOW

Soon after William was born, Liv and Kurt moved into The Lakelands, their dream neighborhood. It was a self-contained neighborhood that had a Main Street with restaurants and shops. There was also a diner, movie theater, ice skating rink, mini golf course, grocery store, and a Home Depot. Liv loved taking William up to the neighborhood pool and to the playground in the spring and summer months. Liv, Kurt, and William had all made many great friends in The Lakelands. Life was good.

In less than three years, they had moved twice. Their current home in the Lakelands was over 4,000 square feet and was set on Inspiration Lake. The house was three stories high and was yellow with black shutters. On the top floor, there were three bedrooms, two bathrooms, and the laundry room. On the second floor was a two-sided, woodburning fireplace, family room, gourmet kitchen, dining room, office, sunroom, and formal living room. Attached to the kitchen was an expansive mahogany deck that overlooked the lake. The first floor had a spacious toy room for William, a fourth bedroom, a steam room, and a wine cellar for Kurt's growing wine collection. On the back of the house was a slate patio that looked out onto the lake with a beautiful lawn complete with a rose garden and a three-tiered fountain.

So how did Kurt and Liv end up in this incredible home? Well, they had actually lived in the house next door for a year and a half. Their first home in the Lakelands was 2,500 square feet with four bedrooms and four and a half bathrooms with a woodburning fireplace. But every night, Kurt would pull down the driveway in his red Porsche Carrera and dream of living in the house on the lake. Liv, on the other hand, was very content with their current home. But one night, Kurt just couldn't take staring at the house next door anymore. He parked his Porsche in the garage, then marched over, and rang the Baxter's doorbell. The Baxters, who lived in the home, were in their sixties, and Kurt thought that they might be ready to downsize. After an hour of negotiation, Kurt made Mr. Baxter an offer that he just could not refuse. Kurt ran back home to tell Liv the good news!

"But Kurt, we just finished redoing the kitchen, toy room, and our master bath! Do we really need a house that big? And besides, can we even afford it?"

"Liv, my business is doing great and, yes, we can definitely afford it. Stop worrying and start packing. We move in at the end of the month." By this point in their marriage, Liv had learned that when Kurt really wanted something, there was no talking him out of it. One month later, they were living next door in their dream house on the lake.

Once they moved in, Liv was ecstatic. She redid the kitchen, master bath, and the entire basement. She hired an artist to paint murals in the dining room, sunporch, and William's room. She took great pride in their new home.

So, you're probably wondering, how did Liv and Kurt go from eating out of their vegetable garden to living in this grand home? It was all due to Kurt's ambition. He had acquired a very high-powered client at Goldman Sachs who had wanted to start his own private equity firm for the extremely wealthy in the DC area. He made Kurt a partner at the firm. And after two years of running the firm, Morgan Stanley bought them out. After that, Kurt went on to work for an IT company that was based out of India. Then he bought the *Cigar Aficionado* magazine of Washington, DC. That's where things really started to get interesting. Kurt and three other partners, who had also worked at Goldman Sachs, started traveling to China. They put their heads together and decided to buy the country's airwaves. The Chinese didn't have cell phones yet, but when they wanted them, they would need Kurt's company in order to get them. In addition to all of that, Kurt had been hired by the Pentagon as an independent defense advisor. He had made a lot of friends on Capitol Hill and his future looked brighter than ever.

Now, to be honest, Liv's parents and family members were all very concerned. Everyone in Liv's family had all been working at Gallagher Construction for generations. They couldn't understand how or why Kurt changed jobs so frequently. But, Liv's family also couldn't deny that he was providing Liv and William with a pretty extraordinary lifestyle. Kurt had kept his promise. Liv had a full-time housekeeper and a part-time nanny. She drove a Mercedes SUV. William attended a private school—Christ Episcopal School. They were members of the Saint Francis Episcopal Church in Potomac and the Congressional Country Club. They had a full social calendar which included political events, supper clubs, and charity fundraisers. Their Christmas party had become the biggest holiday event of the season. Every year, a full catering team would transform their home into a winter wonderland. The guests were greeted at the door by men in tuxedos handing out green and red martinis. The outdoor deck was tented and the dinner menu was

always very extravagant. Kurt even dressed up as Santa Claus every
year and handed out a personalized gift to every guest.

Kurt and Liv had come a long, long ways. It seemed for Kurt
and Liv as if 'they had the world on a string and they were both
sitting on a rainbow.'

CHAPTER 27

HOW DOES THIS KEEP HAPPENING?

May 24th, 1998. Kurt, Liv, and William were just leaving their Sunday church service at St. Francis and heading over to the Old Anglers Inn Restaurant as they did on most Sundays for brunch. As they walked across the church parking lot, Liv said, "Kurt, my allergies are really bothering me. I think I'll run into CVS to get some allergy medicine."

"Mom, are you okay?" asked William.

"Of course. It's just that time of year. Go with your dad and I'll meet you at the car. I'll just be a minute."

Once Liv was in the CVS, she went straight to the family planning aisle and grabbed a pregnancy test. *I can't believe this might be happening again*, she thought to herself as she made her way up to the register. After paying for the test, she slipped it into her purse.

The family had brunch and afterwards, when they arrived home, Kurt and William went upstairs to change out of their church clothes. Kurt always liked to do yard work on Sunday afternoons. Liv went into the powder room and opened the pregnancy test. She peed on the stick and waited, and within three minutes, the test confirmed that she was pregnant once again. *Oh, boy*, she thought. Coming out of the powder room, she saw Kurt sitting on the sofa putting on his sneakers.

"Where's William?" asked Liv.

"He's playing in the yard."

"Kurt, I have to tell you something." Liv pulled the test out from behind her back and handed it to Kurt.

"You're pregnant?!" he said. "Again? How did this happen? I feel like every time I look at you, you get pregnant! I honestly can't believe this!"

"I honestly can't believe *you!*" said Liv. "You're acting like you had nothing to do with this!"

"Liv, we had a deal. One child."

"Kurt, we never had a deal, and let's face it, we haven't been very careful. And, by the way, I think it would be nice for William to have a brother or a sister."

"You're unbelievable," Kurt said, grabbing his keys and storming out of the house. Liv could hear his Porsche racing up the driveway.

William ran into the house. "Is everything all right, Mom? Where's Dad going?"

Liv sat down on the sofa. "Everything's fine. Just go back outside and play. I'm going upstairs to change my clothes and give Nana a call."

Liv put on her sweats and called her mother.

"What are you all up to on this beautiful Sunday?" her mother asked.

"Well, we went to church this morning and brunch, as usual. Oh, and by the way, I'm pregnant."

"What?!"

"Yes, mother. I'm pregnant again. I honestly don't understand how this keeps happening."

"Liv, you said the exact same thing the last time this happened. Don't you and Kurt know anything about the birds and the bees? So what did Kurt say?"

"He's very upset and he's acting like this is all my fault."

"Well, that's just completely ridiculous. He'll be all right, Liv. He just needs a little time."

"Mom, when you tell your husband that you're pregnant, you don't expect him to storm out of the house."

"Liv, Kurt is a great father to William. He'll be fine. You'll see."

"I hope you're right, Mom."

"I'm always right, Liv. Haven't you figured that out by now?"

"Well, you're not always that funny, Mom. I'll talk to you later."

Liv hung up the phone and went downstairs to start Sunday dinner. At 6:30, the usual time, she put dinner on the table. But there was still no sign of Kurt.

"William," she said, "go wash your hands and come sit down at the table. Dinner's ready."

"But where's Dad?" William asked.

"He had to go to his office for a while, so it's just me and you tonight."

After dinner, William went downstairs to play in the toy room. Liv was cleaning up in the kitchen and loading the dishwasher. She heard the front door open. Kurt walked in with a dozen pink roses.

"I'm sorry," he said, handing Liv the flowers.

Liv took them and sat down at the kitchen table. "Kurt, sit down. We need to have a talk. Every time we have a problem, you can't just take off like that. It's not fair. I want us to be a team and work out our problems together."

"I know, and I'm sorry. I was just in shock. I feel like we have the perfect life, you know?"

"Well, this baby is just going to make it that much better. You'll see. I love you."

"I love you too, Liv. Always and forever." He kissed her and said, "So, when do you think this baby is coming?"

"I'm guessing January."

"So we're having a Christmas baby?"

"Yes, we are," she said, smiling. "We're having a Christmas baby."

CHAPTER 28

THE ICE STORM BABY

January 1st, 1999. What a year it had been. Liv's due date was January 15th. Her second son was almost here. That's right. Liv was having another boy! William couldn't wait to meet his baby brother and, yes, Kurt was very excited about the baby as well. But he did say that this would be their last child. He had even gone so far as to schedule a vasectomy for mid-March. Liv was very upset about the vasectomy and was secretly hoping that Kurt would change his mind about having more children. This pregnancy had been a breeze compared to William. She had very little morning sickness and was full of energy. She had even been running three miles every day throughout her pregnancy. The only complaint that she had was that she was craving Mexican food all the time. Thank God there was a Baja Fresh in the neighborhood.

January 14th. William had just taken a bubble bath and was sitting by the fireplace with Buddy watching "SpongeBob SquarePants." Liv was in the kitchen trying to decide what to make for dinner. Just then the phone rang. It was Kurt, reminding Liv he was going to be late. He had a business dinner in downtown DC that evening.

"But are you sure you can't make it home for dinner?" Liv said.

"Liv, I told you, this is a very important meeting. We're having dinner with a potential investor at The Palm."

"I know. I guess I'm just a little nervous. It's starting to snow and they're predicting a blizzard by morning."

"Liv, I promise to get out of here as soon as I can. Oh, and by the way," Kurt added, laughing, "don't even think about having this baby tonight!"

"Ha ha, very funny," Liv said. "I actually feel fine. I'll probably be late again just like I was with William. Well, good luck with the meeting, and please drive safe!"

After they hung up, Liv called for William who came running into the kitchen. "Your dad has a meeting tonight so he won't be coming home for dinner. So why don't you and I have a make-your-own-pizza night?"

"Yes!" answered William as he ran to the fridge to gather up all of the ingredients. Make-your-own-pizza night was a big hit in the Donovan household.

Liv preheated the oven then glanced out of the window. "Look, William, it's really starting to snow." William ran over and looked out of the kitchen window. The deck had at least an inch of snow on it already.

"Wow! Mom, look at it! Do you think that I'll have school tomorrow?"

"I don't think so. It's really coming down out there. Come on, let's set the table and decide what toppings to put on our pizzas."

Around 9:00 p.m., Liv tucked William into bed and said prayers with him. As she pulled his blinds down, she looked up the driveway. The snow had begun to change over to ice. The roads are going to be a mess, she thought. She walked into her bedroom just as the phone rang. It was Kurt.

"I'm in the car and I'm on my way home," he said.

"Well, that's good. It looks really bad out there. The snow is starting to change over to ice. So please be careful driving. And I really think you'd better park your car up at the street. If you try to pull down the driveway, you might never get it out tomorrow."

"Okay. Don't worry, I'll be home soon. Love you."

"Love you, too."

When Kurt got home, he kissed Liv on the cheek. She was already fast asleep. Liv slept soundly until about 7:30 the next morning when she awoke with the unmistakable discomfort of labor pains.

"Kurt, wake up!"

"Huh? Liv, we can sleep in. School has been canceled for today." Kurt rolled back over.

"Kurt! I'm having contractions!"

"What? Are you sure?"

"Of course I'm sure."

Kurt sat up and he and Liv began timing the contractions. Liv picked up the phone and called her doctor. "Dr. Conlen, it's Olivia Donovan. I've been having contractions for about an hour now and they're four minutes apart."

"Olivia," said Dr. Conlen, "do you realize we're having the worst ice storm in Washington DC history?"

"Well, what are we supposed to do?"

"Stay calm and don't panic. First things first. I'll try to get to the hospital, but it doesn't look good. We lost power at my house in the middle of the night. I really can't leave my wife and four kids here with no power. But don't worry. I'll put a call into our practice and one of the doctors will meet you at the hospital."

Liv hung up and said, "Kurt, we need to get to the hospital."

"Okay, I'll call Misty and Charlie next door and ask if they can come over to watch William." Then Kurt watched as Liv went into the bathroom and turned on the shower. "Liv, what are you doing? We don't have time for you to take a shower."

"Kurt, the last time this took hours. I think we have time. Now, go wake up William, take him downstairs, put on *Bear in the Big Blue House*, and give him a cereal bar. Then give Charlie and Misty a call."

"Okay, whatever you say. But please hurry!"

After Liv showered, she picked out a nice pair of cozy pajamas, put on her robe and slippers, and headed downstairs.

"Liv, why aren't you dressed?" said Kurt.

"Kurt, they're just going to make me change as soon as I get to the hospital."

Misty and Charlie rang the doorbell just then and Kurt let them in.

"Well, isn't this an exciting morning?" smiled Misty. "Liv, isn't today your actual due date?"

"Sure is. This one's right on time! Oh my gosh, I have to call my parents."

"Liv, we really need to get going," said Kurt.

"Okay, okay, well, grab my suitcase and go warm up the car. I'll only be a minute."

Liv went into the kitchen and called her parents.

"Liv, why are you calling so early? Is everything alright?," her mother said.

"Well, Mom, it looks like I'm in labor. We're heading to the hospital now."

"Liv, I hope you're joking. Do you know how bad this ice storm is? They're saying this is the worst winter storm since 1979. Millions of people are without power."

"So I've been told, Mother. Look, I have to get going. I'll call you from the hospital."

Liv's dad grabbed the phone before Liv could hang up and said, "Liv? You're really in labor? Victoria, what are you doing?"

Liv heard her mother tell her dad, "If my daughter is going to have a baby, I'm not going to miss it."

"But, Dad, tell Mom that the roads are awful!"

But all she could hear was her mother yelling at her father in the background, "Peter, get dressed! We're going to Maryland!"

"Hang in there, Liv. We're on our way!" her father said

"But, Dad," she said, but there was nothing but a dial tone. "Oh, brother."

Liv walked back out to the living room and saw William watching TV. "William, come sit on the couch."

"Okay, Mom."

"Listen, William, I have to go to the hospital now because your baby brother is coming today."

"Oh, wow! I'm finally going to get to see him."

"Yes. I'll have someone bring you over right after he's born."

"Charlie and I would be happy to bring him over, Liv," said Misty.

"Great. Thanks so much for helping out."

Kurt came in the front door just then. "Okay, the car is running, but Charlie, can you please help me get her up the driveway? It's like an ice skating rink out there."

Twenty minutes later, they finally got Liv up the driveway and safely into the car. Kurt looked over at her and said, "I told you that you couldn't have the baby today." They both laughed as Kurt pulled out and began driving toward the hospital.

CHAPTER 29

MY TWO SONS

By the grace of God, they somehow managed to make it to the hospital. The roads were a sheet of ice and they were littered with accidents. Liv's contractions were now coming one on top of another.

"Kurt, I can't walk. Please go inside and get me a wheelchair."

Kurt pulled up to the emergency room entrance, jumped out of the car, and was back within minutes with a wheelchair. He wheeled Liv into the hospital, forgetting to turn off his car.

"Hi, I'm Olivia Donovan and I'm going to have a baby. Like right *now*," said Liv to the woman sitting behind the desk.

"Okay, who is your doctor?"

"Dr. Conlen."

"Oh, yes. He called in about you. Give me your wrist. I need to put your ID bracelets on and, sir, can you please go and park your car?"

"Oh my gosh, yes," said Kurt. "Of course."

"We're going to take your wife up to room 313. We'll meet you up there."

Once up in the birthing suite, Liv changed into a hospital gown and a nurse came in to take her vitals. "Where's my doctor?" Liv asked the nurse.

"Don't worry. The doctor is on the way. This winter storm has made everyone late today."

Kurt walked into the room and started unpacking Liv's suitcase. "I can't believe this, Liv. I forgot the camera!"

"What? Are you sure?"

"Yes, it's not in here."

"Sir," the nurse said, "we sell disposable cameras in the lobby's gift shop."

"Great," said Kurt. "Liv, I'll be right back."

"Kurt, you better hurry," Liv called after him as he sped out of the room.

"Okay, well, I have to go tend to my other patients," said the nurse.

"But, wait. I really want an epidural."

"Honey, we need the doctor to order that. Don't worry. I'm sure the doctor will be here soon." Then the nurse left, shutting the birthing room door.

Soon, the pain was becoming unbearable for Liv.

"Oh my God," she exclaimed, hitting the call button on her bed. "I'm in room 313 and I really need help."

No response.

"Hello, is anyone there? I really need a doctor."

Still no response. Liv suddenly realized she was all alone in the hospital room. *I can't have this baby by myself.* All of her manners went straight out the window. She hit the call button again and screamed, "What the fuck is going on?! I'm about to have a baby! I need help *now!* Where the hell is everyone?"

Just then, Kurt swung open the door. "Liv, I could hear you screaming all the way down the hall."

"Well, where is my doctor?"

"The hospital is understaffed today because of the storm."

"Kurt, I need you to listen to me, okay? This baby is coming!"

Kurt lifted up the sheet. "Oh my God, I see the top of his head!"

"Kurt, go get help!"

Kurt took off running down the hall and shortly reappeared with a young, curly, red-headed woman.

"Hi, Olivia. I'm Dr. Friedman and I'm going to deliver your baby today."

"Is this some kind of joke? You look like you're twelve."

"Well, I'm not twelve, I can assure you. Now, let's take a look. Okay, you are definitely ready to push."

"Wait one minute! I need an epidural. You can't expect me to deliver this baby without any kind of medication."

"Olivia, we don't have time for that. This baby is coming out."

The doctor called over the intercom and within minutes the room was full of doctors and nurses.

"Why are there so many people in here?" said Liv. "I didn't have this the last time I gave birth."

"Dr. Conlen has written in your chart that you might be having a preemie. His notes say that you have only gained fifteen pounds during your pregnancy." She then placed Liv's feet in the stirrups. "Okay Liv, give me a nice big push."

"Oh my God! Get him out!"

"That's good. Another one just like that. His shoulders are out. I just need a couple more good pushes."

Kurt looked at Liv and said, "You can do this."

"Okay." She pushed two more times and the baby was out. The medical staff slowly began leaving the room.

"Is everything okay?" said Liv.

The doctor lay Liv's new baby boy on Liv's chest.

"Wow, he's huge," Liv said.

"Eight pounds, seven ounces," said Dr. Friedman. "This is no preemie."

Liv looked down at her son. He was breathtaking. He had brown, reddish hair, an apple-shaped face, and piercing blue eyes like Kurt's. His thighs were huge with yummy baby rolls. He looked up and smiled at her.

"Oh my gosh, Kurt. He's beautiful." Then she looked up to see her parents coming through the door. "Mom, Dad, you made it!"

"There was no stopping your mother. Liv. She was on a mission."

Liv's mom threw her purse down. "Let me hold my new grandson." Liv passed the baby over to her mother. "Liv, he's gorgeous. He looks like the Gerber baby."

"You'll never believe this, Mom, but they thought he was going to be a preemie."

"A preemie? He looks like a linebacker to me!" Liv's dad said.

"Oh, Mom, let Kurt hold the baby. With all of the excitement, he hasn't even gotten a chance to hold his son."

Liv's mom gently placed the baby into Kurt's arms. Kurt had tears running down his face. "Well, Liv," he said, "what shall we name our second son?"

"I think we should name him Jeffrey Gallagher Donovan after my great, great-grandfather."

"Well, Jeffrey," Kurt said, looking at the baby, "you sure did pick quite the day to make an entrance into the world." Then glancing over at Liv, he added, "I think we should refer to him as the ice storm baby."

Just then, William, Misty, and Charlie burst into the room. William was dragging a huge teddy bear behind him, a gift for his new baby brother.

"I'm sorry, we just got tired of waiting at the house," said Charlie.

"Is that my brother?" William said.

"It sure is," said Kurt.

"I want to hold him."

"Come sit next to me and you can hold him." William sat next to his father and Kurt slid the baby onto William's lap.

Jeffrey smiled at his big brother and William giggled. "I think he likes me."

The nurse came in and offered to take a few photos. "Yes, please," said Liv, but she knew she wouldn't need photos to remember this day. It would be etched in her memory forever. And on that snowy winter's day in January, all seemed to be right in the world.

CHAPTER 30

THE WORLD WAS
THEIR OYSTER

July 4th, 2001, Sea Island, Georgia. Liv, Kurt, William, and Jeffrey were back on Sea Island to celebrate the Fourth of July. Liv had come to the island as a child, but the year after William was born, they started coming back as a family. The entire Donovan family was in love with this tiny island off of the coast of Georgia.

They would spend their days taking long walks on the beach, looking for sand dollars, swimming in the warm Georgia sea, and riding their bikes under the canopy of giant oaks that lined the streets. The salt air and the Southern charm of Sea Island had captivated all of them.

July 4th morning always started off with the "All-American Parade" down Cloister Drive with magnificent floats, decorated bicycles, and vintage cars. After the parade, there was an afternoon of family pool games, a Southern barbecue lunch, and the very patriotic children's bathing suit contest. William and Jeffrey had entered wearing matching American flag swim trunks. Kurt, Liv, William, and Jeffrey were the portrait of the all-American family.

But a lot had happened since Jeffrey's wintry birth two years before. Kurt had been 100 percent right about his China airwaves venture. In the fall of 1999, the Chinese wanted cell phones and they needed Kurt and his partners to get them. He and his partners ended up selling their company to China Unicom for twenty million dollars. That left Kurt with a cool four million in the bank. So, he decided to start his own company called Eagle's Armor. He would now go after large government contracts, filling orders from everything from flashlights to gun slings to bulletproof vests. Kurt was hoping that the relationships he had built at the Pentagon and Capitol Hill would make his new company a huge success.

With his new wealth, Kurt also went on a shopping spree. He bought a 458 Ferrari Spider that was midnight blue with beige interior. He signed up for Net Jets, vowing never to fly commercial again. In Kurt and Liv's wallets were brand-new black American Express cards. And for Liv's thirtieth birthday, Kurt surprised her with an oceanfront condo right next door to The Breakers Hotel in Palm Beach. They were, as Liv's grandmother Dovie would have said, "living high on the hog."

After a long day of Fourth of July fun and the extravagant buffet dinner at the Sea Island Beach Club, Kurt, Liv, William, and Jeffrey all gathered down on the beach to watch Sea Island's spectacular fireworks display. As they all gazed up at the night sky, each burst of fireworks just kept getting better and better. Just like each passing year that Liv and Kurt had been together. It definitely seemed at the moment that for Liv and Kurt, the world was their oyster!

CHAPTER 31

WEDDING BELLS

September 8th, 2001. Baltusrol Country Club. Liv, Kurt, and William walked through the main lobby of the club out to the open-air slate patio where the wedding reception was being held for Liv's cousin Russell, and his new bride Holly. It was a black tie affair. Even William was wearing a tuxedo. They decided to leave Jeffrey at home since this was going to be a very late evening. All of the Gallaghers were thrilled to welcome Holly into their family.

Liv, Kurt, and William found their table for the reception. At their table were Liv's parents, Liv's sister Sarah, and Sarah's fiancé, Robbie. Yes, Sarah was getting married! Sarah and Robbie had grown up together at the Jersey Shore but they'd lost touch when they had both gone off to college. After college, Sarah, who had studied at the Fashion Institute in New York City, was now working for a small custom bridal shop in Spring Lake, New Jersey. One Friday after work, she was meeting a group of friends for happy hour at the Parker House in Sea Girt. It was there that she bumped into Robbie. They were both so happy to have run into each other that they exchanged numbers and, as they say, that was that.

Robbie and Sarah had gotten engaged the previous October on Sarah's birthday. With Liv and her mother's help, Robbie had picked out an exquisite emerald-cut diamond ring from Tiffany's. Liv finally had the brother she had always wanted. Robbie was sweet, smart, funny, and had a heart of gold. He had a real love for family, golf, and the Jersey Shore. At the table, he turned to William and said, "The next wedding you'll be at is ours." Then he leaned over and kissed Sarah while William giggled.

The waiters soon came with the entrees: rack of lamb with mashed potatoes and green beans. William looked down at his plate. Robbie leaned over and said, "Not exactly kid food, is it? Let's go into the kitchen and see if they can make you something else." William took Robbie's hand and followed him into the kitchen. In a moment, they returned.

"They're going to make me chicken fingers and french fries," said William.

"Thank you, Robbie," Liv said.

"No problem. He needs a good meal before he hits the dance floor." They all laughed. "And William, I promise at *our* wedding to make sure you have whatever you want for dinner." William gave Robbie a high five.

After dinner, they all hit the dance floor dancing to "We Are Family." It was a great wedding. At midnight, they all said their goodbyes and piled into the limo, which took them to Liv's parents' house where they all stayed that night.

The next morning, Liv walked into the kitchen to make coffee and noticed a box of hot donuts from Donuts Plus in Lavallette. Next to the box was a note. *Had a great weekend. Love, Robbie.* Liv opened the box as Kurt, William, and Jeffrey came into the kitchen.

"Wow, donuts!" William cheered. "I bet they're from Uncle Robbie."

"They sure are," Liv replied. "Okay, get some paper plates and we'll have breakfast out on the deck."

Sarah walked into the kitchen with her suitcase. "I can't believe you're leaving so early," said Liv. Their cousin Jill had been killed in a horrific automobile accident the week before in Tennessee and Sarah had agreed to go to the funeral to represent the family.

"I know," said Sarah, "but it's not easy to get to Johnson City. I have a connecting flight through Pittsburgh. I'll go say goodbye to the boys and Kurt. Where's Mom and Dad?"

"They're still sleeping. I guess all that dancing wore them out. Well, safe travels, sister. Love you," Liv said as she hugged her sister.

"Love you, too."

CHAPTER 32

THE DAY THE WORLD WOULD CHANGE FOREVER

The morning of September 11, 2001. Liv was in the kitchen finishing her morning coffee and packing William's lunchbox. Jeffrey was in his highchair, happily enjoying a bowl of Cheerios, and Kurt was in the laundry room looking for matching socks as always.

"Liv," he said, "I just don't understand why I have a whole drawer of dress socks and none of them match."

"Darling, I've been hearing this for the last seven years."

"Well, if I can't find a matching pair, I'm going to be late for my meeting at the Pentagon this morning."

Liv walked over to the staircase and yelled up the stairs to William. "Let's go, William. We're going to be late for school."

"I'm coming, Mom."

Liv lifted Jeffrey out of his highchair. "Say bye-bye to Daddy."

Kurt gave Liv and Jeffrey a kiss as William ran into the kitchen and grabbed his backpack. "By, Dad," he said, "see you at dinner."

"Have fun at school," said Kurt.

And with that, Liv and the boys were out the door. Liv put the boys in their car seats and then stopped to look up at the sky. Wow, what a beautiful fall day, she thought. The air was crisp and there wasn't a cloud in the sky.

It took Liv over an hour to get William to school every morning due to the terrible traffic on the beltway. To pass the time in the car, she'd listen to music and to the outlandish DC morning radio talk shows.

After battling the morning traffic, she finally pulled into the carpool line at Christ Episcopal school. As William got out of the car, Liv said, "Have a great day. Love you."

William turned around and waved to his mom.

Liv and Jeffrey were finally back on 270 North heading home. Liv turned the radio on to listen to one of the sports radio talk shows and heard the typical sports banter: "Can you believe how bad the Redskins are this year? The Chargers killed us on Sunday thirty to three. It's outrageous! Daniel Snyder paid $800 million for what? A bunch of bums! Anyways, speaking of bums, looks like some idiot in a commuter plane just flew into one of the Twin Towers in New York City. I wonder where he got his pilot's license? I'm guessing out of a Cracker Jack box!"

Were they kidding? Liv thought. *That really isn't funny.* She hit scan on the radio and stopped when she heard, "If you're just joining us this morning, Matt Lauer has just announced that the North Tower of the World Trade Center was hit by an aircraft."

Liv's heart began to race. She drove home as fast as she could, pulled down the driveway, got Jeffrey out of his car seat, and ran into the house. She went into the living room and turned on *The Today Show*, stunned by what she saw. Smoke was billowing out of the North Tower. She ran to the kitchen to call her mom.

"Mom, what's going on? I'm watching *The Today Show*."

"Your sister's a mess," said her mom.

"This is unbelievable, but thank God Robbie's not there." (He had been working the Asian market at Carr Futures for the last month, so he wasn't usually there during the day.)

"He is today, Liv. *Robbie is there.*"

Liv felt like she was going to vomit. "Mom, what are you talking about? That can't be."

"Your sister spoke to him at 8:15 this morning. Someone called in sick so he's covering for him."

"Oh, God, no, Mom," said Liv. "Where's Sarah?"

"She's stuck at the Pittsburgh airport waiting for her connecting flight to Newark. Let me call you back. She's calling me now."

Liv sat down on the couch and stared at the TV, unable to believe Robbie could actually be in that burning building. And then the unthinkable happened. A second plane flew into the South Tower. *Oh, my God. What is going on?*

Liv ran back into the kitchen and called her mom. "Mom, did you see that the South Tower was just hit?"

"Liv, your sister just got off the phone with Robbie. They're trying to get out of the building but the stairwells are full of smoke and fire. Liv, the president has just made an announcement. This was a terrorist attack. Where's Kurt?"

"Oh my God, Mom, he's at the Pentagon!" Just as she spoke those words she heard Matt Lauer report that, "At 9:37 this morning, there was a huge explosion on the western facade of the Pentagon. They now believe that the Pentagon has also been hit by a plane."

Liv tried calling Kurt's cell phone. No answer. She kept trying.

At 9:59, she watched as the South Tower collapsed.

The phone in the kitchen rang. Liv picked it up and heard Kurt's voice. "Liv, oh my God."

"Kurt, are you okay?"

"Yes."

"Kurt, what is going on?"

"The United States is officially under attack."

"Kurt, I need you to go and get William."

"Liv, all of the schools are in lockdown."

"Kurt, I need my son and you home! Please, I'm begging you!"

"Okay. Try to stay calm. I promise you I'll go get him."

Liv hung up the phone, grabbed Jeffery, and went into the garage to put him into his jogging stroller. She was numb and in shock. All she wanted to do was run. She started running around the lake. As she was running, she prayed, "Please God, please let Robbie be okay. He has to be okay."

"Liv," came a voice. "Liv, stop!" She turned to see her neighbor, Misty. Liv stopped running. "Liv, I went over to check on you. Your phone kept ringing, so I answered it. Your mom wants you to call her right away."

"Misty," said Liv, "Robbie's in the North Tower."

"I know. Your mom told me. Where's Kurt?"

"He's going to get William from school."

As they walked back into the house, Liv looked over at the TV. The North Tower had collapsed.

"Go call your mom," said Misty, "and I'll take Jeffrey upstairs to get him ready for his morning nap."

On the phone, Liv's mom said, "Liv, I've decided to drive to Pittsburgh to get your sister. All of the flights in the US have been grounded. Sarah shouldn't be alone at a time like this. She's completely hysterical. Where is Kurt? Is he okay?"

"Yes. He's going to get William from school."

"Thank God. I'll call you later today."

Liv hung up and walked over to turn the television off. Misty walked into the living room.

"I'm going back to my house now," she said. "If you need anything, just give me a call."

"Thanks," Liv said, and the two hugged.

Liv went upstairs and peeked into Jeffrey's room. He was fast asleep. Then she went into the bathroom and turned the shower on. Tears began to run down her face. She knew in her heart that Robbie was gone. She got dressed and went downstairs just as Kurt walked into the house with William.

"William!" Liv said. William ran into his mother's arms. "Thank God you're home," Liv said, then looking up at Kurt, added, "both of you." Liv was overcome with gratitude to be holding her son in her arms and looking at her husband. She thought of all the wives who had lost their husbands, and mothers who had lost their children on this catastrophic day in September, a day that would change the world forever.

CHAPTER 33

ROBBIE IS NOT GONE... WE JUST CAN'T HUG HIM ANYMORE

September 28th, 1:00 p.m. The Church of the Presentation in Saddle River, New Jersey.

Kurt, Liv, and her parents walked down the center aisle of the church and joined Sarah in the first pew on the right side of the church. Liv turned around and saw every single member of her family in attendance. Liv and Kurt had decided not to bring William. Ever since 9/11, William had been having terrible nightmares about buildings collapsing and bad men. Liv told William that sometimes there are actual angels on earth and Robbie was one of them. Robbie had to go up to heaven, she told him, to be with all of the other angels. But he would forever be in their hearts.

Robbie's family was seated across from them in the first pew on the left side. This was the church where Robbie and Sarah would have been married. But instead of wearing a white wedding dress, Sarah was wearing a black dress suit.

The church was packed. They had even set up giant jumbo screens in the parking lot so people could watch the service. Over a thousand people came to pay their respects that day. Liv was struck by the utter sorrow and surreal atmosphere of the occasion. On the altar were a few bouquets of white roses and white lilies, but in lieu of flowers, Robbie's family had asked for donations to the widows and children's fund for the Uniformed Firefighters Association. There was no casket. There was no urn. Robbie's body had not been recovered from Ground Zero. Instead, there were huge pictures of Robbie on the altar. My God, thought Liv, he was so very young and so incredibly handsome.

Liv flipped through the funeral program. On the back page was a black and white photo of Robbie at the shore, standing on the deck staring out at the ocean. Under the photo was a passage:

Perhaps they are not stars, but rather openings in heaven where the love of our lost ones pours through and shines down upon us to let us know they are happy.

Her eyes welled up with tears. She looked over at Kurt. He put his arm around her and kissed her cheek.

The priest soon came out and everyone rose. There were prayers and tears. Robbie's brother, Mikey, spoke first about his big brother and how he had the biggest heart out of anyone he had ever known. He spoke of Robbie's love of golf and how you could find him on the golf course with his father every Friday afternoon. And no matter how bad the traffic was in the summer months, Robbie would battle it to enjoy his weekends at the Jersey shore with his family, friends, fiancée, and his dog Daisy.

His sister, Jeannie, spoke next. She told the story of how when Robbie was heading to the airport to go off to Ireland, Daisy tried desperately to get into the car to go with him. They were inseparable.

Robbie spent hours on the beach throwing Daisy a tennis ball in the surf. "My brother loved many things. Bon Jovi—I can't even begin to tell you how many times he went to see them in concert at Giants Stadium. And yes, the Giants were his favorite football team of all times. Every weekend in the summertime, he would go down to the Seaside Boardwalk and bring home a pizza from the Sawmill. It was his favorite, but he would always say that nothing could ever compare to our mom's cooking. Especially her homemade tomato sauce with Italian sausage and peppers. Sunday dinners on the deck were some of the most special times for our family. We are all so very grateful that we were together on the Sunday before 9/11. We had no idea that would be the last time that we would all see Robbie."

Robbie's father, Dr. Zampieri, then spoke. He told the congregation that Robbie was not *gone*, that Robbie would never be gone. It's just that he couldn't hug his son anymore. And with that, all you could hear were sobs throughout the congregation. He then asked for everyone to please pray for the Vialonga family. He explained that Chris Vialonga was a longtime friend of Robbie's. They had attended Bergen Catholic High School together and Chris was the one who got him the job at Carr Futures. They had even shared a desk together. "So now we all have two angels looking down upon us," he said. He then spoke of Robbie's love and devotion to Sarah and how she would always be a part of their family. Liv reached over and squeezed her sister's hand.

Dr. Zampieri concluded by asking everyone to pray for peace, and not to carry hatred around in their hearts regarding that horrific September day. He ensured the congregation that Robbie was at peace and he was now with the Lord. The service ended with the Lord's prayer and then the priest asked everyone to recite this prayer by Helen Lowrie Marshall:

I'd like the memory of me to be a happy one.
I'd like to leave an afterglow of smiles when life is done.
I'd like to leave an echo whispering softly down the ways,
Of happy times and bright and sunny days.
I'd like the tears of those who grieve to dry before the sun,
Of happy memories that I leave when life is done.
Amen.

It was an emotional and touching memorial. The Zampieris were a very strong Irish Catholic family, and Liv could see through all of their pain and grief that their faith was something to aspire to. Her sister, Sarah, also amazed her by her strength and grace in the midst of this unimaginable tragedy.

After the service, there was a reception. Sarah, along with the Zampieris, personally greeted and thanked every single person for coming.

When they finally returned to Liv's parents' home at the shore, all of the Gallaghers gathered on the deck to watch the moon rise over the ocean. They ate pizza from the Sawmill, drank red wine, and told their favorite Robbie stories. Robbie was gone, but he would never be forgotten.

Not ever.

CHAPTER 34

"ROBBIE'S DAY"

Sunday, September 11th, 2005.

It was hard to believe that Robbie had been gone for four years. Kurt and Liv had decided that on every September 11th, they would take the day to remember him. If there was school, the boys would stay home. Liv referred to this day as "Robbie's Day." Liv, Kurt, William, and Jeffrey would spend the day as a family doing things that Robbie loved to do. They would drive out to the Eastern Shore of Maryland, listening to Bon Jovi and Bruce Springsteen along the way. They would always go to the same restaurant on the water in St. Michaels, The Crab Claw. There they would dine on oysters on the half shell, steamed, and fried. Robbie had loved oysters. The boys would feed dried corn to the ducks off the dock. Then they would all go into Christ Church and say a prayer for Robbie and light a candle.

Before heading home, they would put their car on the ferry that would take them over to Oxford, Maryland. In Oxford, they would walk along the sandy cove and look for sea glass. Robbie had a gift for finding sea glass. During the summer, in Jersey, he would spend many afternoons on the beach with William looking for sea glass. One day, Robbie had given Liv a piece of red sea glass. Liv had been collecting sea glass her entire life but she had never found a red one. She cherished it and hoped that one day she might find a red piece herself.

The day would end by stopping at the Oxford Town Park where the boys would throw the football with Kurt just as they had done with Robbie at the shore. Robbie had been convinced that Jeffery was going to be a star football player one day. Liv would laugh and say, "Stop that, Robbie, he's only three for heaven's sake." Finally, they would get into their car for the two-hour-long ride home.

Liv always hoped that Robbie would have been happy by the way they had chosen to remember him. This year, as they drove over the four-mile Chesapeake Bay Bridge, Liv reflected on the last four years. Both of Kurt's grandparents had passed away, so Liv's family was all the family that Kurt had. He never did speak to his mother again after the incident at their wedding. Liv's sister Sarah had gone into a deep depression after 9/11 and had moved back in with her parents.

As for Kurt's business, it was better than ever, but he was gone a lot. Liv thought he was gone too much. He'd be away for three weeks and then home for two, traveling the world attending every military trade show that he could. He had missed all of Jeffrey's birthdays. This was definitely not the marriage Liv had envisioned for herself. She had tried to talk to Kurt about his absence on many occasions, but his answer was always the same: "Things are going to get better, Liv. You'll see." But so far, they hadn't. Liv often felt as though she was raising the boys alone. They were the loves of her life. William was observant, clever, and caring. Jeffrey could light up a room with his big smile and loving personality.

To pass the time when Kurt was gone, Liv had started a small catering company out of the house. She focused on small dinner parties, birthday parties, and luncheons. Kurt found this to be appalling.

"I can't believe you've become a servant to our friends and neighbors!" he told her. But Liv didn't care what he thought. She always felt that busy was better, and she was having a ball catering the parties.

She also had gone back to teaching, becoming a substitute teacher at William and Jeffrey's school. She loved being back in the classroom, but this, too, didn't sit well with Kurt.

"You only make $100 a day teaching," he said to her. "I'll give you $100 a day to stay home and take care of our family." Kurt seemed embarrassed by Liv's working. He felt that he was providing her with a lifestyle that few women could ever have and she should just appreciate it. But this was not who Liv was. Worse, Kurt had gone through with the vasectomy. This broke Liv's heart. They were both still so very young and Liv felt that the vasectomy was a huge mistake.

As they pulled into their neighborhood, Bruce Springsteen's song "Waiting on a Sunny Day" was playing on the radio. Liv hoped that one day Kurt would see that he was missing precious time with her and the boys. She hoped that things would get better. If Robbie's death had taught her anything, it was to appreciate and enjoy each day because it truly is a gift. Surround yourself with the people you love and never miss the opportunity to tell someone that you love them. *Love you Robbie*, she thought. *Always*.

CHAPTER 35

THAT'S IT! WE'RE MOVING TO FLORIDA

Winter 2005. Kurt, Liv, William, and Jeffrey boarded their private jet to head down to Palm Beach for the boys' winter break. Tragedy had struck the Gallagher family once again. Liv's grandmother, Dovey, had passed away and six months later, her grandfather had passed, as well. The family all felt that he had died from a broken heart. Liv's heart was broken, as well. She missed her grandmother every day. Dovey was her idol. She wanted nothing more than to be just like her grandmother and to make her proud. Dovey was the glue that had held the Gallagher family together over the years. To keep her grandparents' memory alive, Liv had decided to host a New Year's Eve party at The Breaker's Hotel for the family. So, on December 27th, the entire Gallagher clan checked into The Breakers.

Over the next two weeks, the family enjoyed their time together on the beach swimming, building sandcastles, and playing touch football. Liv knew that her grandparents would have been overjoyed to know that the family was all together again at The Breakers, this special place where they had all been coming to for generations.

After two weeks of family fun, the Donovans headed home to Maryland. As they pulled down the driveway, the first thing they noticed was that their house was completely dark. As they all stepped out of the limo, Kurt said to Liv, "Stay here with the kids. I'll go inside and grab some flashlights."

Kurt returned with the flashlights and then they all went into the dark house.

"Liv, wait here with the boys. I need to go downstairs to check the fuse box," Kurt said. As soon as he reached the bottom step, he shouted, "Oh my God, Liv! I can't believe this!"

Liv ran over to the staircase. "What's wrong?"

"The entire basement is flooded! A pipe must have burst. Stay upstairs! The water is up to my knees. The entire basement is ruined. The toy room, wine room, bathroom, everything!" Kurt came back upstairs. "I can't believe this happened. Do you know how much money we've spent on finishing that basement? That's it, we're moving to Florida!"

"I don't want to move to Florida," said William.

"Me, either," said Jeffrey.

"Calm down, boys. Let me talk to your father. Here, take my flashlight and go up to your rooms. Put your PJs on and I'll be up in a minute to tuck you both in." The boys went upstairs and Liv turned back toward Kurt. "Kurt, what's wrong with you? Have you completely lost your mind? We can't just pack up and move to Florida!"

"Liv, I can run my business anywhere. You know that. I'm telling you, call the realtor tomorrow. We're putting the house on the market. Besides, I don't even know why you're arguing with me! You hate the cold weather and you love Palm Beach."

"Kurt, just because I hate the cold doesn't mean we should just pick up and move. Plus, we have homeowners insurance to cover the water damage in the basement."

"Liv, you're not listening to me! The Donovans are moving to the Sunshine State!! And that's final!"

CHAPTER 36

WELCOME TO PALM BEACH

Much to Liv's surprise, it had only taken two weeks to sell their home in the Lakelands. Liv had to admit it was one of the prettiest houses in the neighborhood, and there had even been a bidding war over their home. Kurt was ecstatic and couldn't believe he had more than doubled his money on the sale of the home. So that was that. The Donovans were moving to Palm Beach.

The following weekend, Liv and Kurt flew down to Palm Beach to meet up with Liv's Aunt Charlotte. Aunt Charlotte was currently on her third husband and had several important connections in the Palm Beach area. Aunt Charlotte and Liv's new uncle, Duke, had a penthouse in New York City, a house in Grosse Pointe, Michigan, and a house in Palm Beach. Aunt Charlotte promised to help Kurt and Liv find the perfect home, as well as the ideal school for William and Jeffrey.

The house-hunting weekend was very successful thanks to Aunt Charlotte and her very good realtor friend BeBe Wagner. Liv and Kurt had fallen in love with a magnificent home on Seaspray

Avenue. The home was over 8,000 square feet with eight bedrooms and six and a half bathrooms. It had a chef's kitchen, formal dining room, great room, library, and two fireplaces. The backyard had a beautiful swimming pool with a spa and a covered porch with a gas fire pit. The landscaping was gorgeous, with bougainvillea, royal palms, and a fifteen-foot high ficus hedge that surrounded the entire property.

Walking around the house with Bebe and her aunt, Liv said, "Kurt, do we really need a house this big?"

Kurt pulled her aside. "Liv, I know you're going to want your family to come down to visit often. And besides, I've been thinking, you're really not that happy with our lives in Maryland."

"Now, Kurt, I wouldn't go that far."

"Liv, please just let me finish. I want this to be a fresh start for all of us. And to tell you the truth, you were right. I never should have gotten the vasectomy."

"Kurt, what are you saying?"

"I'm saying, Liv, let's fill this house with children. Lots and lots of children."

"Kurt, are you sure?"

"Yes, Liv. All I've ever wanted to do was to make you happy. So what do you say?"

"I say yes!" She grabbed Kurt and gave him a big, long kiss. And then she kissed him again.

Kurt walked over to the realtor. "Well, Bebe, we'll take it. We absolutely love the house!"

"Great! I'll have the papers drawn up and sent over to you by this afternoon. Congratulations! To both of you! And welcome to Palm Beach."

CHAPTER 37

"SEA DREAMS"

O n May 1st, 2006, the Donovans moved into their new Florida home and were officially residents of the Sunshine State. Liv wanted the boys to have one month at their new school to make friends and get acclimated before the summer vacation started. Thanks to Liv's Aunt Charlotte, William and Jeffrey had been accepted into the Palm Beach Country Day School. Aunt Charlotte had even helped to get Kurt and Liv a family membership at the exclusive Palm Beach Bath and Tennis Club. As Liv's grandmother Dovie would have said, "When you walk through the lobby of the club, you could smell the money— the old money, that is."

The entire family was thrilled with the move. William and Jeffrey had already made some new friends at school and in their new neighborhood. Liv loved the fact that the boys could be outdoors all the time, shooting hoops, riding their bikes, playing touch football, and enjoying the beach. They had even started playing lacrosse with some of the neighborhood kids and were excited to try out for the school's team in the fall.

Kurt was on cloud nine with the move. He was enjoying the status of the B&T membership and of his new address on the island of Palm Beach. He even had a mahogany sign made for the house that read, "SEA DREAMS." Kurt was also delighted that he had found an office with warehouse space that was only twenty minutes from their new home. Business was good, but he wanted to expand his company. Kurt had decided that he wanted to start going after large law enforcement orders as well as government contracts. He also wanted to start producing his own line of bulletproof vests, helmets, gloves, pistol pouches, luxury luggage, backpacks, and medical pouches. Kurt was a very busy man, but he did promise Liv not to travel as much, and he was also trying to make family dinners his number one priority. Kurt was finally putting his family first, and there was even some talk about having another baby in the Donovan household.

CHAPTER 38

THE BOY NEXT DOOR

Christmas Eve, 2006. The Donovans had decked the halls and were very excited about celebrating Christmas in their new Florida home. Liv's parents and sister had flown in the day before and the rest of the Gallaghers would arrive in time to celebrate New Year's Eve.

The boys were loving Palm Beach Country Day. The school's curriculum was challenging, but they both received all A's and B's in their first semester. William and Jeffrey also made the fall lacrosse team and were enjoying their newfound love of the sport. The boys had formed many new friendships, but Austin Davis, the boy who lived two doors down, was by far their favorite.

Austin was somewhat of a golf prodigy and held the title of Junior Champion for the state of Florida. A few years earlier, when Austin was just eight, Matt Lauer interviewed him on *The Today Show* due to the fact that Austin had recently won the US Kids' Worlds. William and Jeffrey decided to take up golf, with Austin's assistance, of course. Austin possessed the patience of a saint and enjoyed taking them golfing. Unfortunately, Austin didn't get a lot of time off due to his touring and practice schedule. He also was currently attending the International Golf Academy in Bluffton, South Carolina. But he was always able to come home around Christmas for three weeks.

The family attended the Christmas Eve church service at 4:00, and then returned home for an elegant dinner. Liv was overjoyed to have her whole family together once again. After dinner, they all went up to their bedrooms to change into their matching Christmas pajamas. Then the family gathered around the fireplace to hang their stockings and listen to Liv's father read his rendition of "The Night Before Christmas." After the boys set out a letter for Santa, along with cookies and milk, Liv and Kurt tucked them into bed and said prayers. Shortly afterwards, Liv's parents and sister also decided to turn in for the evening. Liv and Kurt headed downstairs to open a bottle of champagne and to get their "Mr. and Mrs. Claus" duties underway.

As they listened to Christmas carols and put tinsel on the tree, there was a loud knock at the front door. Kurt opened the door to find Austin on the doorstep. He had a huge black eye and was crying. Liv glanced at Kurt and then walked over and put her arm around Austin and said, "Austin, why don't you come into the kitchen with me and let's put some ice on that eye."

While Liv was tending to Austin, Kurt decided to walk down to the Davis's home to find out exactly what had happened. He knocked on the door and Heather Davis opened the door immediately, stepped outside, and then closed the door quickly behind her. "Merry Christmas, Kurt."

"Thanks, Heather," replied Kurt. "Look, I came by to speak to you about Austin's eye."

Heather looked down at the ground and then said, "I'm afraid Mark is under a lot of pressure at work. He just has a lot on his plate right now and he's not handling it very well."

"I see."

"To be honest, Kurt, with everything that's going on, I was wondering if Austin could stay at your house for the remainder of his winter break."

"Heather, you know Austin is always welcome at our home and, of course, he can stay with us."

"Thanks, Kurt, I really appreciate your kindness and understanding."

"Anytime." Kurt walked back to his house, not fully understanding what was going on in the Davis's household, but knowing that Austin was better off staying with them, at least for the time being. When Kurt got home, he pulled Liv aside and explained the situation. She also agreed that Austin should stay with them.

Liv took Austin upstairs to one of the guest rooms and got him settled in. "So, Austin, your mom said it would be okay for you to stay here with us for a while. Is that okay with you?" Austin nodded. "Okay, well, please try to get some sleep. Tomorrow's a big day and I'm sure Santa will be bringing you a lot of presents."

Liv joined Kurt back downstairs in the living room. "So, what are we going to do?"

"About what?" said Kurt.

"Santa is coming tomorrow. Austin needs to wake up in the morning and find gifts under the tree."

"Right. Well, all we need to do is take some gifts from William and some from Jeffrey and rewrap them. You always buy them way too much anyways."

"Great idea. I'll go grab the wrapping paper."

At sunrise, Jeffrey burst into his parents' bedroom yelling, "Santa came! Santa came! Mom, Dad, get up!" "

"Okay, Jeffrey," said Kurt. "Go get everyone up and we'll meet you at the staircase." Liv smiled and put on her Christmas robe and slippers.

At the staircase, the whole family lined up according to age, oldest to youngest (a family tradition), including Austin. As they all descended down the staircase, it was clear that Santa had definitely found the Donovan's new home. All three boys ran to the tree and began opening their presents. Kurt put his arm around Liv and said, "Once again, you've turned a house into a very special home. Love you."

"Love you, too. Merry Christmas."

CHAPTER 39

"WELCOME HOME, SON"

July 2007. Once again the Donovan family was back at their favorite vacation spot: Sea Island, Georgia. Liv was on her morning beach walk, taking in the sights and sounds of the island. The sun had just begun to rise above the horizon. The warm Georgia sea rolled in calmly over her toes and the sandbars went on for miles. The salt air was briny and smelled divine. The sandbars went on for miles. This was Liv's favorite time of the day. The boys and Kurt were out on their morning bike ride around the island. Austin would be arriving that afternoon. He had just finished competing in the Future Masters Golf Tournament in Dolan, Alabama. As expected, he took first place. He was clearly becoming a rising young star in the golf world.

Over the past few months, Kurt and Liv had learned a great deal more about the Davis family. First off, Austin was an only child. Sadly, Heather and Mark had been battling a serious drug and alcohol addiction for years. There had been multiple DUIs, arrests, and long stays at several rehab facilities. It truly was a miracle that Austin had turned out as well as he did. Liv and Kurt both felt that golf had saved him. It kept him busy, focused, and, most importantly, out of his dysfunctional household.

Kurt could certainly identify with Austin's family struggles. As for Liv, it was very difficult to watch Heather and Mark's downward spiral. Mark was forced to declare bankruptcy and Heather lost her teaching position having failed one too many drug tests. The bank had foreclosed on their home and they were living on what little savings that was left. The couple was so clearly overwhelmed with their own problems that Austin had been pushed aside. Kurt and Liv were happy to pick up the pieces and welcome Austin into their family. He fit seamlessly into the Donovan household and the boys had even embraced him as a brother.

As Liv turned around to start walking back to their oceanfront villa, she thought back to Easter weekend. On Easter morning, there was the traditional Donovan Easter egg hunt in the backyard for the boys, followed by the ten o'clock church service, then Easter brunch at the Bath and Tennis Club. The rest of the day was spent on the beach swimming, sailing, and throwing the football. That evening, they all gathered around the dining room table to enjoy the Easter dinner that Liv had prepared: deviled eggs, honey ham, macaroni and cheese, creamed spinach, and homemade buttermilk biscuits.

Austin said, "Mrs. Donovan, may I please have another biscuit?"

"Of course," Liv replied, as she passed him the basket of biscuits. "Austin, we need to have a little talk." Liv put her arms on the table and folded her hands together. "So, I've been thinking. Since you're going to be living with us, I think we need to come up with a name for you to call me. Mrs. Donovan is much too formal. Don't you agree? I thought maybe you could call me Olivia, or Liv, or well, anything that you're comfortable with is fine with me, Austin. So, do you have any ideas?"

"That's easy. I already know what I want to call you."

"You do? Okay, what did you have in mind?"

"Mom. I want to call you Mom."

Liv's eyes welled up with tears. She glanced over at Kurt and her boys. "Austin, are you sure?"

"Yes, I'm very sure. I really don't ever want to go back to living with my parents. I want to stay here with you guys. I do hope that one day my parents will get their lives together but…"

"But what, Austin?" Kurt asked.

"The thing is, you all feel like the family I've always wanted."

"So, I guess it's all settled then," said Kurt.

"Austin, will you please come over here and give your mother a hug?" said Liv.

Austin got up and ran around the table to hug Liv. "Happy Easter, Mom."

She looked at Austin and said, "Welcome home, son."

And that's how Liv became a mother for the third time. In life, some things are just meant to be.

CHAPTER 40

SECOND THOUGHTS

Liv had been anxiously awaiting this day for years. Kurt was scheduled to have surgery at Boca Regional Hospital that morning to reverse his vasectomy. Liv's heart was full of excitement and joy.

She was making their bed, eagerly waiting for Kurt to finish getting dressed so they could be on their way. Kurt walked into the bedroom wearing his gym clothes and sneakers.

"Are you ready?" Liv asked. "Now, listen, don't be nervous. Dr. Larson said this procedure is a piece of cake and you know I'm going to take the best care of you."

"Liv, I just got off the phone with Dr. Larson's office."

"Why? Is everything okay?"

"Yes. But I've changed my mind."

"About what?"

"I decided to cancel the surgery."

Liv felt her heart drop. "What? Why on earth would you do that? You know I want to have another baby more than anything in the world! Kurt, that's one of the reasons we bought this huge house. I don't understand. How could you do this to me?" She sat down on the bed feeling defeated.

"Listen, Liv, I've been thinking about this a lot. You know how I've been traveling to China for years."

"Yes, Kurt. How could I forget? What does that have to do with us having another child?"

"Remember how I told you when I would stay at the Marriott in Guangzhon that I would see the families lining up every morning to go into the ballroom to meet their adopted children for the first time?"

"Yes, but I'm still not following you."

"Well, I've come to the conclusion that's what I want us to do!"

"So let me get this straight. Now you've decided on your own that you want us to adopt a child from China?"

"Yes, Liv, I want us to make a difference in a child's life just like we're doing for Austin."

"Kurt, this makes no sense. People adopt children because they're unable to have their own. That's not the case for us. We are capable of having more children if you would just go through with the surgery today."

"Liv, if you could only see the joy on the faces of those families. I'm telling you it's a beautiful thing."

"I'm sorry, Kurt. I just don't feel the same way about adoption as you do. And I also can't believe you waited until the morning of your surgery to tell me all of this."

"Liv, I really wish you could understand where I'm coming from, but I'm definitely not going to change my mind on this one." He walked over to the dresser and picked up his keys.

"So, that's it?" said Liv. "You're leaving?"

"I'm going to the gym and then to work." And with that, Kurt turned and walked out of their bedroom.

Liv was furious and in a state of total shock and disbelief. Once again, Kurt had made a decision without discussing it with her first. *He's unbelievable,* she thought. *What kind of marriage is this, anyways?* She tried to calm down, but she was enraged. She also had no doubt that there would be a very expensive piece of jewelry or an over-the-top vacation heading her way. That was Kurt's solution to every disagreement that they had ever had. He always felt that he could just buy his way out of any argument.

Liv thought back to the night that she first met Kurt and how he said he never wanted to get married or have children, how he wanted to spend his life serving his country and traveling the world. Ever since their move to Florida, Kurt had very slowly begun to travel again. She thought maybe this was her fault, maybe she was trying to change him into someone he simply wasn't. Maybe he couldn't be the man she wanted and dreamt of her entire life.

Liv knew that she still loved Kurt and she wanted more than anything to keep their family together. She remembered what her grandmother once told her, that marriage was a roller coaster ride. There would be good years and bad years. She also had made a promise to Kurt and had taken vows before God. And even though she was tremendously disappointed in him, she also felt as though she had no choice but to stay in the marriage. She did hope and pray that, someday, things between them would get better. But deep in her heart, she wondered if they ever would.

CHAPTER 41

LITTLE PALM ISLAND

As Liv predicted, Kurt planned a lavish thirty-fifth birthday getaway weekend for her. He was whisking her away in a seaplane to the exclusive Little Palm Island Resort in the Keys. Liv had heard many great things about the resort and was looking forward to a relaxing weekend. On Friday morning, they drove down to the Boca Aviation Airport and boarded a seaplane.

Liv was very excited. She had never been on a seaplane before. Once they took off, they flew down the coast of Florida over Miami and then over Stiltsville, a group of wooden, stilt houses that were built in Biscayne Bay, some of which had been there since the 1930s. Soon, they were over the Everglades, and then they finally made their way down to Little Palm Island. They flew around the island three times before landing in the sea and then docking. Liv loved every second of the flight.

When they climbed out of the seaplane, a resort staff member was there to greet them on the dock with mimosas. "Good morning, Mr. and Mrs. Donovan. I hope you enjoyed your flight. My name is Blair and I would like to welcome you to Little Palm Island. Is this your first time staying with us?"

"It is. I've been wanting to come here for years," Liv replied.

"Great. Well, please follow me and I'll give you a quick tour of the property. As you can see, there's a walking path that runs in a circle around our little five-and-a-half-acre island. We have thirty thatched roof villas, all with outdoor showers, and each with its own private beach and firepit. We have two restaurants and we also serve dinner on the sandbar nightly, weather permitting, of course. Oh, and please don't be surprised by the Key deer. They roam about the island and are completely harmless. On the dock, we have a dozen Boston Whaler boats at your disposal, and we can also provide you with fishing and diving equipment, as well. Across from the dock is our world-class spa. And I understand that it's someone's birthday this weekend."

"It's my birthday tomorrow," Liv said.

"Well, you've definitely come to the right place to celebrate and I do believe your husband has a few romantic surprises planned for you this weekend. Okay, so here we are. Villa number three. Come on in and let me show you around." They stepped inside to find a tropical living room, a beautifully appointed bathroom with a soaking tub, and a luxurious outdoor shower. In the bedroom was a four-post bed covered in a sheer white mosquito net. The entire bungalow screamed romance. "All right then, I'll leave you two to get settled. If you need anything at all, please let our staff know."

Kurt pulled out a twenty-dollar bill and thanked Blair. "Oh, one more thing before you leave," he said, "what's the Wi-Fi password and how's the cell service on the island?"

Blair smiled. "Mr. Donovan, we don't allow the use of cell phones on the property and we also don't have TVs or Wi-Fi. Little

Palm Island was created to allow you to experience nature and focus on enjoying each other. Now, I hope you two have a lovely afternoon." And with that, she let herself out.

"Liv," said Kurt, "did she just say there's no Wi-Fi or cell service on this island?"

"Yes, Darling, I believe she did," Liv smiled.

"And no TVs?"

"No TVs."

"Liv, you know I have a lot of work to do. And what about Sunday football? The Redskins are playing the Cowboys."

"I don't know what to tell you, dear, except that so far, this is turning out to be a great birthday. What do you say we put on our bathing suits and go get some lunch at the beach restaurant? I'm starving." She opened up her suitcase and pulled out her bathing suit and coverup.

Over lunch, Liv suggested that she thought it would be fun to do some fishing in the afternoon.

"Olivia, I've been married to you for eleven years now and I've never seen you catch a fish."

"Well, Mr. Donovan," replied Liv, "you'd be surprised to know all of my many talents."

Kurt and Liv enjoyed a beautiful lunch and then got set up for an afternoon of fishing off the dock. Much to Kurt's surprise, Olivia caught three nurse sharks. He, on the other hand, caught nothing. After fishing, they went back to their bungalow to take a nap before dinner. Except neither of them slept. They spent the afternoon making love in the outdoor shower.

At sunset, they left their bungalow and followed the path that was lit by tiki torches to the restaurant. The hostess greeted them and said, "Mr. and Mrs. Donovan, if you will please follow me, your table is ready." She led them out of the restaurant and around the corner to a private beach. There was a path of red rose petals leading the way to a table set for two.

"Wow, Kurt," said Liv, "this is beautiful and look at that amazing sunset."

"I'm glad you like it," Kurt said, pulling out a chair for her. "I wanted to do something memorable for your birthday."

Liv sat down and took the menu the hostess handed her. Printed at the top it read: "Happy 35th Birthday, Liv!"

"Kurt, this is spectacular," she said. "Thank you so much. Today was perfect. And I love that you never stop surprising me after all of these years."

"Olivia, I know that I don't tell you this often enough, but I'm so grateful that you married me."

The waitress brought over a bottle of champagne and filled their glasses. Kurt raised his glass and said, "Happy birthday to my beautiful wife." They toasted and sipped the champagne. He then pulled out a Tiffany's box from his pants pocket. He placed the box on Liv's dinner plate.

Liv carefully opened the box. Inside was an exquisite, eighteen-karat gold and platinum leaf ring covered in round diamonds.

"Kurt, my God, it's gorgeous!"

"Just like you," Kurt said. "Here, let me help you put it on."

"I really don't know what to say, Kurt."

"I want you to say that you won't give up on me or us. I want you to know how very much I love you and our family."

Liv looked down at the ring and thought about all of her many blessings. Life with Kurt definitely hadn't been easy, but she loved him and was grateful for their three beautiful sons. She raised her glass and looked into Kurt's eyes. "Cheers to celebrating many more birthdays together."

Olivia Whittaker wasn't going anywhere. She was one 100

percent committed to her marriage. And she also knew life is so much brighter when you focus on what truly matters and, in her case, it was her family.

CHAPTER 42

A FACE OF AN ANGEL

Liv put the pot roast on the stove and turned the heat down to a slow simmer. She then put on her pink Lilly Pulitzer sweater and was out the door. She loved the fact that the boys' school was only a five-minute walk from their house. The days of sitting on the beltway stuck in commuter traffic were long gone. It was a brisk November afternoon and Liv was grateful that she was only wearing a sweater instead of a huge down winter jacket.

When she arrived at the Palm Beach Country Day School, she raced across the school's parking lot. She didn't want to miss one second of Jeffrey's basketball game. His team was playing against Benjamin to see who would move on to the playoffs. Jeffrey was the point guard on the team. He was having a fantastic season and was leading the team in points scored. Every time he made a basket, he would point at Liv in the stands. She would always point back at him and cheer, "That's my baby!"

Liv slowed her pace down when she reached the sidewalk leading to the school's gymnasium. All of a sudden, she felt a small hand slide into hers. She looked down and, staring up at her, was a beautiful little Asian girl with the face of an angel. Liv knelt down and said, "Hi, sweetheart, are you lost?" Liv guessed that the child was about three. "Where's your mommy?"

Liv stood up and saw a blond-haired woman streaking toward her yelling, "Joy, wait. Joy, I'm coming!" When the woman reached Liv, she scooped the little girl up in her arms and said, "Joy, I was so worried. You can't wander off like that, sweetheart." Then she turned to Liv and said, "Hi, I'm Kim Saddler. I am so sorry. We just adopted her from Vietnam two weeks ago and we're all still getting adjusted. I think she saw your blond hair and she thought you were me. Again, I'm really very sorry. Come on, Joy, let's go watch your brother play basketball."

Liv smiled as the pair walked into the gymnasium.

At home over dinner, Jeffrey recapped the game for the family. Jeffrey's team had won in overtime, with him scoring the winning basket. When the boys had finished, they cleared their dishes and then went upstairs to start their homework.

Liv told Kurt about the event at school with the little girl. "Kurt, my heart melted when I saw that little face and when she was holding my hand, I realized something."

"Realized what?"

"Well, it just felt right. It felt like…I don't know how to say this except it felt like she could have been my daughter."

"Liv, I don't think I'm following you."

"Kurt, I've changed my mind."

"About what?"

"I think we should adopt a child from China."

"What? Are you sure?"

"Yes, I'm very sure. I'm going to start researching the foreign adoption process tomorrow."

Kurt's eyes welled up with tears. "Liv, you have no idea how happy I am," he said. "And you'll see. I truly believe this is God's plan for us." Then he leaned across the table, kissed her, and said, "Liv, you definitely have the world's biggest heart. That's one of the things I love most about you. So, I guess our little family of five will soon be a family of six, after all."

Liv smiled and kissed him back. "I really hope so."

CHAPTER 43

SHE KNEW IN HER HEART HER BABY WOULD COME FROM THAT WONDERFUL ISLAND

Over the next week, Liv focused on learning all she could about the foreign adoption process. She discovered that the first step was to complete a home study. (A home study is done by a certified social worker to ensure that a child is placed in a suitable home.) After spending many hours on the computer and conducting numerous phone interviews, Liv decided to hire Charlotte Peyton to prepare their home study. Charlotte was a social worker with excellent credentials and she also specialized in foreign adoptions.

In their lengthy phone conversation, Charlotte explained to Liv what was required in order to execute a home study. She also told Liv that the adoption process was a lot like giving birth. "The labor part—going through all the paperwork, red tape, and waiting for your child—is very painful," she said, "but the birth is when you finally hold your child in your arms and you realize that it was all worth it."

Charlotte asked Liv what country they were thinking about adopting from. Liv explained Kurt's ties to China, and the many reasons they both felt strongly about adopting from that country. There was a long pause at the other end of the phone and, finally, Charlotte asked, "Liv, do you know what the Hague Convention is?"

"No," Liv replied. "I've never heard of it."

"Well, it's an international agreement that addresses child trafficking. It provides standards to safeguard against illegal adoptions. China and several other countries aren't part of the convention. I'm sorry to tell you this, but you and your husband won't be able to adopt a child from China. But don't worry. There are so many children around the world that need good homes. I suggest you take a look at the Hague Convention Act and choose another country and then we can go from there."

"Okay," Liv said, stunned by the news. She knew Kurt had his heart set on adopting a child from China. "Let me speak to my husband and I'll get back to you."

Liv hung up the phone and went straight to the family's computer to read all about the Hague Convention. Then she picked up the phone and called Kurt at work. "Kurt, I have good news and some not so good news."

"Okay, what's the good news?" Kurt said.

"Well, I found the perfect woman to do our home study for us. She has a lot of experience and is an expert in foreign adoptions."

"That is good news. So what's the bad news?"

"Well, it turns out that we can't adopt a child from China." Then Liv went on to explain what she'd learned.

"Liv, this can't be."

"I'm afraid at this point in time, there's no way we can adopt a child from China."

"But, Liv, I only want to adopt a child from China. You know that."

"I do know that, but we're going to have to be open to adopting from another country."

"Listen, Liv, I have to get back to work. Let's talk about this tonight over dinner. I love you."

"I love you, too."

Liv got back on the computer and pulled up a list of the participating countries in the Hague Convention. Then she Googled a map of the world. She kept staring at China. Then she noticed that off the coast of China was the island of Taiwan. She called Charlotte back immediately. "Charlotte," she said, "can a US couple adopt a baby from Taiwan, even though Taiwan is technically under the Republic of China?"

"Actually, yes," said Charlotte. "In fact, I just did a home study for a couple that is adopting from Taiwan."

"Do you remember what adoption agency they used?"

"Hold on, let me look that up for you. Oh, yes, it was the Gladney Center for Adoption. They're based out of New York City. Here's the number. You should give them a call and ask about their Taiwanese program. I'm sure they'll be able to answer any questions that you might have."

"Thanks, Charlotte. This is great news."

Liv stared at the computer screen and at the island of Taiwan. She knew in her heart that her baby was going to come from that wonderful island.

CHAPTER 44

FULL STEAM AHEAD

Over the course of the next year, Liv was overloaded by everything that was required for their foreign adoption. Kurt and Liv had decided to enroll in Gladney's Taiwanese Adoption program, since China was no longer an option. There were thirteen other families in the program. The agency explained to all of the families that it could take a year, or possibly two, to go through the entire adoption process. First, there was the home study to complete, then over twenty hours of online adoption courses. And the amount of paperwork was quite simply overwhelming. This was now Liv's new full-time job.

She was also busy getting the baby's nursery ready. She had hired a very talented carpenter, Bruce O'Connor, and a well-known nursery designer, Betty Davidson, to turn the baby's room into a magical wonderland.

The process of adopting a baby from Taiwan was very unique. The birth mother was given ten family's profiles to look through and then she got to choose whom the adopted parents would be. The profiles included pictures of the potential adopted parents' home, family photos, financial reports, and a very detailed questionnaire. Liv and Kurt were sure that they would be chosen very quickly due to their home, family, and solid financial foundation. On top of all that, Liv was a former school teacher. Who wouldn't choose them? Plus, the baby would have three older brothers to love him or her. Liv and Kurt felt as though they had the perfect family and were extremely confident that, for them, the adoption process would, at the most, take up to a year.

Liv finished the online classes and completed all of the required paperwork in record time. Now, all they had to do was wait.

CHAPTER 45

MEET MS. DEE

And wait they did. Liv and Kurt had completely misjudged the adoption process. Two years had passed and they still had not been chosen by a birth mother in Taiwan.

Every month on the fifteenth, Liv and Kurt received an email letting them know whether or not they'd been selected. Liv would wake up every morning on the fifteenth at 5:00 a.m. and race to the family computer, only to find the same message: "We're very sorry, but we do not have a child that has matched with your family at this time. Please check back next month." Liv would sit in the dark staring at the computer and cry. She didn't know how much longer she could take this heartbreak and disappointment. She'd talk to Kurt about how she felt, but he would tell her to be strong and that it would all work out. "We have to have faith," he would say. "And one day, when the time is right, God will send us our child."

In the meantime, Kurt had gone back to traveling more than ever. His businesses were booming. He had even opened an exotic car dealership. Kurt had always had a passion for cars, so this was a dream come true for him. He explained to Liv that he wanted to travel as much as possible before the baby arrived.

Liv was struggling with all that was on her plate—the adoption, the boys, and keeping up with the house. Kurt decided to hire a full-time housekeeper/nanny to help make Liv's life easier. He hired Dedra Johnson, also known as Ms. Dee. Ms. Dee had been working as a housekeeper on the island since she'd graduated from high school. Her mother and daughters were housekeepers as well. They all had been working on the Island for years for some of Palm Beach's most prominent families.

The first day Ms. Dee came to the house, Liv opened the door to find a six-foot-tall African-American woman dressed in a maid's uniform and wearing glasses.

"Hello," said Liv. "I'm Olivia Donovan. Please come in and I'll show you around the house."

Ms. Dee stepped wide-eyed into the foyer, taking in the enormity of it all.

"Can I get you anything to drink?" Liv asked.

"No, I'm fine," said Ms. Dee. "I just can't believe it."

"What?"

"This house. I've never seen anything like it. It looks like something out of one of my stories."

"Stories?"

"Yes. You know, on TV? *Days of Our Lives, The Young and the Restless, The Bold and The Beautiful.*"

"Oh, you mean soap operas."

"Yes, I guess that's what you white folks call them."

Liv laughed and said, "Follow me, I'll show you around the house."

When they walked into the nursery, Ms. Dee asked, "Are you pregnant?"

"Oh, no, we're adopting a baby from Taiwan."

"Taiwan? Well, that's different. Mr. Donovan told me about the boys and I already know what you're doing for Austin. You're a real good woman, Mrs. Donovan."

"Oh, please, call me Liv. Or Olivia."

"Well, Miss Olivia, you have a good heart and you're so pretty. Mr. Donovan is one lucky man."

"So you'll take the job?" asked Liv.

"Of course," said Ms. Dee. "I'll work Monday through Friday 10:00 a.m. to 4:00 p.m. But I need to watch my stories and have my lunch every day from one to two, if that's okay."

"That's fine with me. Let me show you out then."

"I think you'd better!" said Ms. Dee. "A person could get lost in this huge house."

Liv laughed. "Come this way."

When they got to the door, she thanked Ms. Dee for coming and walked her out. As she closed the door behind her, she smiled. "I guess angels really do come into your life when you least expect it."

CHAPTER 46

IF YOU LOVE SOMETHING, LET IT GO; IF IT RETURNS TO YOU, IT'S YOURS FOREVER

May 1st, 2009. Kurt was returning home after a weeklong trip up in D.C. on business. On the evening of his return, he had sent a limo to pick up Liv so they could meet at their favorite restaurant in Boca. Liv had no idea what all the fuss was about. Kurt told Liv that his trip had gone extremely well and that he would fill her in over dinner.

As the limo pulled up to Kathy's Gazebo, Liv noticed Kurt was standing outside waiting for her, holding a single red rose. *What on earth?* Liv thought. Kurt opened Liv's door, helped her out of the limo, then handed her the rose and passionately kissed her.

"Wow, Kurt, what is all this?"

"I'll tell you all about it over dinner, my darling."

The maître d' showed them to their usual table. Kurt told the waiter to bring over a bottle of their best champagne and also an order of the Oysters Rockefeller. "We have a lot to celebrate tonight."

"We do? Kurt, what happened up in DC?"

"Well, first of all, you look absolutely beautiful tonight."

"Thank you, but what's going on?"

"So, here's the thing, Liv. While I was in DC, I sort of had a job interview."

"A job interview? For what?"

The waiter arrived with the champagne and the oysters. Liv continued, "Kurt, I don't understand. You're the owner of several successful companies. So why on earth would you need another job right now?"

Kurt whispered in Liv's ear, "The CIA is interested in hiring me."

"Are you serious? For what?"

"Yes, I'm very serious. Liv, as you know, I have a unique military background, top-secret clearance due to the work that I've done at the Pentagon, and impressive connections with high-ranking officials all around the world that took me years to build. They've invited me to go through their two-year training program in Langley, Virginia. After I finish the program, I would be placed in a position where they felt that I could best serve my country. Liv, let's be honest, you know I've always had political aspirations. I truly believe I would make a great congressman, senator, or even governor one day. And let's face it, with you by my side I'm a shoo-in to win any election."

Liv's head was spinning and it wasn't from the champagne and oysters. "Kurt, you're not making any sense. First of all, our family just got settled in Palm Beach. Do you really expect us to move back up north?"

"Of course not. You and the kids don't have to move. I already asked about that. That's why I found an apartment last week in Alexandria, Virginia."

"You leased an apartment?"

"Yes, but don't worry. I get to come home every weekend, Friday through Sunday."

"For the next two years? Kurt, have you lost your mind? This is all too much. And what about me and the kids?"

"Liv, I've thought this all through. You and the kids love Florida and I don't want to disrupt your lives."

"But you've decided to go live in another state without us for two years?"

"Liv, this is a dream of mine that I've had for such a long time. And two years really isn't that long if you really stop and think about it. Besides, you know I've missed serving my country. I almost forgot, there's one last thing. I think you should enroll in their spousal program. If you do, we can live all around the world. Just like Barbara and President Bush did!"

Liv took a big sip of her champagne and then looked Kurt square in the eyes. "Kurt Donovan, if you think I'm going to do some CIA spousal program with you, you're sorely mistaken. I also have zero interest in being married to a political figure. You know my family and I are very private people. And another thing—I have absolutely no desire to live all around the world like the Bushes, so please tell me that you have *not* accepted this position. And, Kurt, before you answer, I do have one last question for you. Have you even considered the baby that we've been waiting to be ours for the past two years?"

Kurt took Liv's hand. "Liv, I'm so sorry you're upset. I never thought you would have reacted this way. I honestly expected you to be excited for the both of us."

"Kurt that's precisely your problem. You never think about me and the kids. You always just think about yourself. Why on earth would I be excited? Excited about you turning our lives upside down once again? I don't think so." Liv felt her eyes begin to well up. "Why Kurt? Why do you always do this? Not only to me but to our children?"

The waiter interrupted to take their dinner order.

"I'm sorry," Liv said. "I'm not feeling very well. If we could please just get the check."

"Of course, right away," said the waiter, hurrying off to get the check.

"I'll be out in the limo," Liv said, and with that she rose and walked out of the restaurant, leaving Kurt alone at the table.

Ten minutes later they were both in the back of the limo heading up A1A toward Palm Beach, neither saying a word. Liv gazed out the window at the ocean and the palm trees dancing in the wind.

Finally, she broke the silence. "So when do you start?" she sighed.

"June 1st," Kurt replied. Then he reached over and grabbed her hand and kissed it. "Liv, in life sometimes, you have to let something go, and if it returns to you, it's yours forever."

She gave him a piercing look. "Yes, but I never thought that that something would be my husband of fourteen years!"

CHAPTER 47

DOES ABSENCE MAKE THE HEART GROW FONDER?

July 4th, 2009. The Donovans were forced to break with their Fourth of July tradition this year. They couldn't spend the Fourth on Sea Island due to Kurt's CIA training schedule. As predicted, he was only allowed to come home Fridays through Sundays, so taking a vacation at this point in time was simply out of the question.

Kurt had been commuting back and forth from Virginia to Palm Beach for a little over a month now. Despite the rigorous training program, he did decide to hold onto his companies in South Florida. He felt as though he had a good team in place and that they could manage without him on a day-to-day basis. Liv, on the other hand, was having a considerable amount of trouble being a weekday single mom. She was now left with the tasks of taking care of the boys and running the household. Thank God for Ms. Dee. Liv knew that without her, she would have never been able to manage all of her new responsibilities. Every Monday, she and Ms.

Dee would divide up what needed to be done around the house and sort out the boys' schedules for the week. Liv's main priority was the boys. She wanted to make sure that their lives remained as normal as possible despite their father's absence.

But keeping it all together was causing Liv constant stress. And on top of everything else, she was missing her husband terribly. She missed having him sleeping beside her, she missed their weekly date nights, and she missed sharing their days over supper. Kurt, on the other hand, seemed fine with the long distance and weekend schedule.

He told Liv, "Listen, it's not going to be this way forever, and I know we'll get through this together."

But Liv felt like she was being pulled in a hundred different directions all at once. She also was having doubts about what this new living arrangement was doing to their marriage and to the family.

Kurt and Liv had been instructed by the CIA to tell their children, family, and friends that Kurt was working once again at the Pentagon on a classified project. Every Friday night at 9:30, he landed at the West Palm Beach International Airport and every Sunday afternoon at 4:30, he'd take the return flight back up to Virginia. He wasn't allowed to tell Liv very much about his training, but she could tell that he was proud to be serving his country once again.

As they sat at their favorite table at the Palm Beach Bath & Tennis Club waiting for the fireworks display to begin, Liv reached across the table and took Kurt's hand. "Kurt, I know it's only been a month, but I'm having a hard time with you being gone and this new schedule of ours."

"I know," said Kurt. "But don't worry. We'll all get used to it. You'll see."

"Kurt, I've also been thinking about the baby. You know I wanted this baby more than anything, but we've been waiting for over two years now, and, with you being gone…"

"What are you trying to say, Liv?"

"Well, I think we should seriously think about withdrawing from the adoption program."

"Are you sure?"

"Yes," Liv nodded.

"Listen, I know I've thrown a lot at you all at once and I understand that you're overwhelmed. But, why don't we give it until August 1st, and if we're not chosen this month, we'll withdraw. Okay?"

"Kurt, I don't think you realize how hard it is taking care of the boys on my own. I really don't believe I could manage caring for an infant right now, with you being gone so much. But I will agree with you not to have us withdraw until next month."

Kurt leaned over and kissed her on the cheek. At that moment, the fireworks display began and the sky lit up with the colors of red, white, and blue. Liv could see her boys running under the lights with sparklers in hand. She was at peace with her decision about the adoption. Now if she could just be at peace in her marriage.

CHAPTER 48

JUST LOOK AT THAT BEAUTIFUL LITTLE FACE

Friday, July 23rd, 2009. Kurt had finished his training early that week and was able to catch the noon flight back home for the weekend. Liv was excited that her husband was coming home early and decided to make a dinner reservation at the club for the Friday night Family Cookout. She was in her bathroom finishing her makeup when Kurt walked in holding a manila folder.

"Don't worry," said Liv. "I'm almost ready. I promise we won't be late. How was your flight?"

"Liv, I have something to show you," said Kurt. He opened the folder and handed her a photo of a beautiful Asian baby. Then he started to cry. "Liv, we finally have our baby."

Liv took the photo and stared at the baby. "This is our baby?"

"Yes. She was born on July 15th. Seven pounds, eight ounces. The birth mother chose us, Liv. We have a daughter!"

Tears streamed down Liv's face. "Oh, Kurt, she's perfect. I love her."

They hugged and Kurt said, "We did it. We finally have our baby."

184

Liv kissed him and said, "Come on, we have to tell the boys."

Liv ran downstairs with the photo in hand. "Boys, come into the living room. Hurry!"

The boys ran in from the backyard. "What's going on?" asked William.

"Your father and I have something to tell you." Liv held up the photo. "This is your new baby sister."

Jeffrey grabbed the photo. "Wow! I'm going to have a sister. She's so small and cute."

"When is she coming home?" asked William.

"Hopefully before Christmas," said Kurt.

"I was hoping for a girl!" said Austin. "No offense, guys. I love you, but I've always wanted a sister."

The three boys all hugged Liv. "I'm the luckiest woman on earth," she said. "Okay, let's finish getting dressed and head on over to the club for dinner."

When the family arrived at the club, Liv couldn't help herself. She showed everyone the photo of her new daughter. She was beaming. She propped the baby's picture up on the table. "I can't believe it finally happened. We have a daughter." Then she reached across the table and took Kurt's hands.

"So, you're happy?" asked Kurt.

"I'm overjoyed. Just look at that beautiful little face. Kurt, you know I've been having my doubts lately, but all that went right out the window the second I saw her face. That's our daughter, Kurt, and as long as we stay strong as a family, I know that we'll get through this. And like you said, before we know it, we'll all be back under the same roof."

"I'm so glad you feel this way, Liv. See? I told you to have faith and it would all work out. So, what do you think we should name our daughter?"

"I was thinking we should name her Rose."

Kurt kissed Liv's hand and said, "What about Rose Olivia Donovan? She should have your name Liv. This never would have happened without your hard work and patience."

Liv nodded with tears in her eyes. She looked up at the full moon and thought of her daughter halfway around the world. *Don't worry, sweetheart, I'm coming to bring you home soon.*

CHAPTER 49

ALL I WANT FOR CHRISTMAS IS TO HOLD OUR DAUGHTER

It was the first weekend in December and Liv was in their library wrapping Christmas presents. She walked over to a pile of gifts that she had purchased for baby Rose. On the top was a Christmas ornament that read, "Baby's first Christmas." Tears began to roll down Liv's face. Just then, Kurt entered the room. He walked over and hugged her.

"I'm so sorry she's not here yet," he said. "We both thought she'd be home for her first Christmas."

"Kurt, it's just not fair," Liv said. "She's legally ours. I just don't understand what is taking so long."

"Liv, the adoption agency explained all of this to us. The adoption is finalized, but we still need the baby's visa to bring her home. Also, I've been wanting to talk to you about something, but I haven't been sure how to bring this up to you because you're already so upset."

"What is it, Kurt? Just tell me."

"It's about the Chinese New Year."

"What about it?"

"Well, it begins on January 20th and it lasts for twenty-three days."

"Okay."

"Liv, I don't think you understand what happens during the Chinese New Year's celebration in Asia. All of the businesses in Taiwan will shut down. Which means, realistically, we probably won't be going to get Rose until March or April."

Liv's stomach turned. "Kurt, all I wanted for Christmas this year was to hold our daughter."

"Liv, you know I've tried everything that I could think of to speed up this process. I've reached out to all of my contacts in Asia and I've gotten nowhere."

"Kurt, how is this going to work exactly with your training schedule? Are you sure you're going to be able to go with me?"

"Liv, they're aware of our situation. I'm obviously not going to get a long period of time off, but they know I have to fly over to Taiwan in order for us to bring her home."

"I'm just worried. The adoption agency told me that if you don't appear at the hearing, her visa will definitely be denied."

"Please don't worry about that, Liv. I want to hold her as much as you do. Now, I have an idea. Let's try to focus on the positive. We finally have our daughter and it's just a matter of time before we can bring her home, right? And we know she's in a good foster home and she's being well taken care of. You have to admit that every time they send us a video, she looks as happy as can be. So, in the meantime, I think we should wrap up all of her gifts and send them to her. I know our hearts are breaking, but let's face it, she doesn't even know it's Christmas."

"You're right. Let's wrap everything up and I'll ship it out to Rose tomorrow. And let's make sure that next Christmas is really special for her."

Kurt laughed. "Liv, with you as her mother, I have no doubt that it will be unforgettable. You, my dear, are the queen of all holidays."

CHAPTER 50

BABY ROSE, HERE WE COME

Sunday, April 19th, 2010. Liv and her mom boarded their China Airways flight bound for Taipei, Taiwan. The flight would be a little over twenty-four hours long with a layover in Anchorage, Alaska. They both sat back and settled into their seats in first class. Liv's mother ordered two glasses of champagne from the flight attendant and then proceeded to show her pictures of Baby Rose.

"Isn't she beautiful?" she beamed to the flight attendant. "We're so excited to be going to Taiwan. My daughter and son-in-law are adopting her."

"Wow, that is exciting! And so very kind of you. There are so many children in Taiwan that need good homes. I'll be right back with your champagne." The flight attendant quickly returned with two glasses.

"Cheers to Baby Rose," Liv's mom said. They clinked their glasses and each took a sip. "Liv, I have to say, I thought this day would never come. I don't think I'll truly believe it, though, until Rose is in my arms."

"Yes, Mother, I'm aware. Remember, you didn't even want me to have a baby shower because you thought it would be bad luck."

"Well, Liv, you have to admit, this process has been heart-wrenching, to say the least, and I must tell you, I think your husband has some nerve sending you and me alone to a foreign country for fourteen days to pick up his daughter. Now, don't get me wrong, Olivia, I know he's always been very good to me over the years, but this just isn't right."

Liv took a giant sip of her champagne. "I know, Mom. I'm so disappointed that he's flying in for less than twenty-four hours to meet Rose and go to the visa office appointment to sign all of the necessary paperwork. I really don't understand him. I'm also tired of trying to make him see that he's missing precious time with me and our children. But I must say, this takes the cake. Well, enough of all that. I just want us to focus on bringing Rose home, okay, Mom?"

"All right, darling, whatever you say. Now, do you have the Ambien that the doctor has prescribed for us?"

"Yes, Mother."

"So, after the dinner service, I think we should take it. It's very important that we both get a good night's sleep."

After dinner, Liv went into the restroom with her carryon bag. She washed her face, brushed her teeth, and put on her cloud pajamas, with her bunny slippers, and hot pink robe.

"Liv!" said her mom when she returned to her seat. "What on earth are you wearing?"

"It's bedtime, Mom, and I want to be comfortable."

"Olivia, you truly are one of a kind."

They both reclined their seats into the bed position and put on their sleep masks. For the next two hours, they both tossed and turned. Finally, Liv's mom said, "Are you tired?"

"Nope," said Liv. "Not one bit. I don't think those pills are working. I think we're both just too excited."

Finally, after twenty-four hours, the plane began its descent into Taipei. Liv had changed back into her clothes, reapplied her makeup, and enjoyed her inflight breakfast. She stared out the window and thought about her daughter, down there somewhere. *Don't worry, Rose. Mommy is coming.*

After Liv and her mom had cleared customs, they made their way to the baggage claim area where they spotted a gentleman holding a sign with Liv's name on it.

He greeted them, "Welcome to Taiwan, Mrs. Donovan. I am Mr. Hong and I will be your chaperone for the entirety of your trip." His English was very broken but Liv and her mom were grateful for his assistance. He gathered up their luggage and ushered them to his minivan.

"I take you now to the Four Seasons?" asked Mr. Hong.

"Yes, thank you," said Liv.

As they drove toward the city of Taipei, it was not at all what Liv had imagined. She had pictured a lush island in the South Pacific. She couldn't have been more wrong. On the outskirts of the city were factory after factory. The city itself had massive skyscrapers that were blanketed in thick smog. The apartment buildings were basic concrete structures with laundry hanging from the balconies. As they entered the city, the streets were choked with traffic. Huge passenger buses that were decorated with fringe curtains weaved in and out, as did numerous scooters, dodging around the traffic at high speeds.

"Wow, Mr. Hong," said Liv, "that looks very dangerous."

"It is," Mr. Hong replied. "Many die every day but it is very expensive to buy a car here in Taiwan."

Finally, they pulled up in front of the Four Seasons. Two bellmen greeted them and helped with the luggage. Liv was relieved that they both spoke perfect English. After checking in, the bellmen escorted them to their rooms. Liv had booked two adjoining corner suites. She walked into her bedroom and saw a gold crib that had been set up next to her bed. She put her hands on the crib and started to cry. Inside the crib was a blanket and a teddy bear with a note that read, "Welcome to the Four Seasons, Rose." *Wow, this is finally happening*, she thought.

"Mom, come see the crib!"

"Oh, Liv, it's perfect. And just think. Tomorrow at this time, my granddaughter will be sleeping right here! Speaking of sleeping, I'm exhausted from that long flight. I really need to go and lie down for a bit before dinner, if that's okay?"

"That's fine, Mom. You go take a nap and I'll meet you at the hotel's restaurant around 6:00."

"Great. This grandmother needs to catch up on her beauty sleep."

At 6:00 sharp, Liv met her mother at the hotel's two-story, open-air restaurant. The hostess showed them to a table on the rail that looked down upon the lower level where there was a stage.

"Excuse me," said Liv to the hostess, "but what's the stage for?"

"Karaoke," said the hostess. "We have the best karaoke entertainment in all of Taipei."

Liv and her mom smiled at each other. "Well, we're definitely not in the States anymore," Liv's mom said.

As they looked over their dinner menus, they were both thankful that the menus were both in Mandarin and English. "Now, Liv, you know I don't care for Asian cuisine."

"No, Mother, I don't know that because you've never even tried it."

"Well, I'm not about to start now."

"Mother, you're being ridiculous. This is probably the best Asian food in all of the world. You should really try it."

Just then, the karaoke began. A young Asian man hit the stage singing the Beach Boys' song *Wouldn't It Be Nice* in perfect English.

"Wow, he's really good," said Liv. The singer waved and pointed at Liv.

"Well, Olivia, it looks like you have an admirer," her mom said. They both giggled.

Meanwhile, they had both noticed a cart being wheeled from table to table. "What's that cart for?" Liv's mom asked.

"I'm not sure. Let's ask the waiter."

When the waiter came over, Liv ordered a bottle of St. Francis Chardonnay and asked about the cart.

"That's our American-style dinner," the waiter explained. "People come from all over Taipei to have that. It's prime rib, baked potato, corn on the cob, and green beans."

"Thank the Lord, I'll have that," Liv's mother smiled.

"Make it two, please," said Liv.

As they sat enjoying the karaoke and their dinner, they both noticed something. The Taiwanese would try to cut the corn like the prime rib and it would roll right off of their plates onto the floor. They didn't know you should pick it up and eat it off the cob. Liv decided to go over to the table next to them to explain how to eat the corn.

"Liv, I must say, ever since you were a little girl, you have always made friends everywhere you go," her mother said.

Liv smiled. "Well, Mom, this has been some day. I can't believe we're finally here. And I don't know about you, but I'm sure that I won't be sleeping at all tonight."

"Me neither, Liv. Me neither."

At 10:00 the next morning, Liv and her mom were back in Mr. Hong's minivan heading to Taichung, where Rose's foster parents lived. The drive was around two hours, and Liv was excited to see more of Taiwan. As they left the city, Liv was surprised how mountainous the Taiwanese countryside was. Along the way, they drove over several bridges, but the rivers below barely had any water in them. There was nothing but large, exposed rocks in beds of mud. Mr. Hong explained that the country was suffering from a terrible drought.

Eventually, they crossed over a set of railroad tracks and entered the city of Taichung. Next, Mr. Hong began driving down narrow back alleys.

"Mr. Hong, where are we?" asked Liv.

"This is where your daughter has been living," said Mr. Hong. Liv's eyes grew wide. There was one concrete building after another with bars covering all of the windows and doors. Mr. Hong explained that this was not a safe part of Taichung. Liv couldn't believe that this was where her daughter had been living for the past nine months.

Liv turned to her mother and said, "Now, Mom, remember what I told you. I don't want us to overwhelm Rose. Don't grab her right away or be overly affectionate."

"I know, Liv. You've explained this to me over and over again, but for the last two years, all I've wanted to do is hold my grandchild! But don't worry, Olivia. I give you my word I'll try to do my best."

Finally, Mr. Hong pulled up in front of one of the apartment buildings. "We're here," he said, as he put the van into park.

As Liv and her mother got out of the minivan, the front door of the apartment building opened. Rose's foster mother stood in the doorway, an Asian woman in her mid-forties with short hair and glasses, holding Baby Rose. Liv nervously tucked her hair behind her ear and walked toward the two of them. When she was in arm's length of Rose, the baby immediately reached out for her. She grabbed Liv's finger and wouldn't let go.

When they entered the apartment, the foster mom instructed Liv to sit down on the sofa. Liv sat in the middle. Her mother was on her right and the foster mom, who held Rose on her lap, was on her left. A woman by the name of Susan was also there. She was an adoption counselor and would be helping to translate and assist in the transfer. The foster mother had typed out Rose's daily schedule. She told Liv her favorite time of the day by far was bath time. She then carefully slid Rose onto Liv's lap. Rose once again grabbed Liv's finger and kept staring at her.

"The foster mother has been showing pictures of you and your family to Rose," explained Susan. "It looks like she recognizes you."

Meanwhile, Mr. Hong was busy capturing this special moment with a video camera and was also taking endless pictures.

Finally, Liv's mom couldn't take it anymore. "Can I please hold my granddaughter?!" she blurted out. Liv carefully passed the baby to her mother. The baby smiled. "Liv, she's so beautiful," her mother said, and then she started to cry. "I'm sorry, Liv, I just can't help myself." They all laughed.

"Well, I think it's time for us to head on over to the baby store," said Susan, "so you can purchase all of the supplies that you'll need for her."

The foster mom hurried into the next room and returned with an armload of packages. It was all of the Christmas gifts Liv and Kurt had sent over for Rose. All were unopened. *That's odd*, Liv thought, but she knew the toys would come in handy back at the hotel. Liv hugged the foster mom and thanked her for taking such great care of Rose.

Rose was wide-eyed as Liv buckled her into the car seat. "She's never been in a car before," explained Susan. "This is going to be a big adjustment for her."

At the baby store, they bought all of the necessities for Rose including formula, baby food, bottles, bibs, spoons, diapers, and clothes. The only clothes Rose had were the clothes on her back. Liv then thanked Susan for all of her help and told her she would see her the following day at the visa office for Rose's appointment.

After about an hour into the trip back to Taipei, Mr. Hong pulled off the highway onto a dirt road.

"Mr. Hong, where are we going?" asked Liv.

"There is a small restaurant in this village that is known for their dumplings and beer," replied Mr. Hong. He soon stopped the van in front of the restaurant, went in, and returned shortly with two cans of beer and three brown bags. "Here," he said, passing back the food and drink. "This is to celebrate your new daughter! It's good luck."

Liv's mom shook her head, but Liv opened the beer and took a sip. "What's in this?" she asked. "It certainly has a different taste."

"It's a mixture of green tea and beer," answered Mr. Hong, starting the van up again and driving on. "It's very healthy. Makes you live for a long time."

"Well, cheers to that, Mr. Hong."

Next, Liv pulled out a dumpling that was the size of a baseball. "Take a bite," said Mr. Hong. "It's a Taiwanese delicacy."

Liv took a small bite. The texture was odd, as was the taste. "It's…interesting," she said. "I can honestly say I've never had anything quite like it. Mr. Hong, if it's not too much trouble, my mother and I really need to use a restroom. Do you think we could stop somewhere?"

"No problem. We're coming up to a rest stop in about fifteen minutes."

At the rest stop, Liv and her mother jumped out with the beer and dumplings hidden in their purses. They walked into the restroom and both gasped. There were no doors, just three stalls with a hole in the ground for each.

"What on earth?" Liv's mother said.

"Look, Mom, we're not in America anymore. So just go with it. And look, there's a trash can over there. We can toss the beer and dumplings."

"I cannot believe your darling husband is missing all of this."

"Okay, Mom, that's enough. Let's get back to Rose."

After another hour of driving, they finally pulled up in front of the Four Seasons. When they got back up to their suite, Liv laid Rose down on her bed. Liv's mom put her arm around her. "Olivia, I think I'll let you have some time alone with your daughter."

When Liv's mom left the room, she stretched out on the bed next to Rose. "Do you know how long I've been waiting to meet you, my beautiful angel?" Tears ran down her face. She kissed Rose on the cheek and said, "What do you say you and I take a bath?"

Liv filled the large soaking tub with warm water and added lots of bubbles. She climbed in holding Rose. Rose splashed and squealed with delight. Liv washed the baby from head to toe. "Don't worry, I got you," she said as she laid the baby on her chest. *What a magical moment and day this has been*, she thought.

Liv had a daughter. In the back of her mind, she had wondered if it would feel any different from the first time that she held Jeffrey and William, but it didn't feel different at all. Except for one thing: she couldn't believe Kurt wasn't there. It was as if he had missed the birth of their daughter. He'd be arriving the following morning. But that could hardly make up for the fact that he'd been absent on this day. It had been a huge day for their family. And, once again, Kurt had missed it.

CHAPTER 51

IT WAS ESSENTIALLY
A CHILD HOLDING A CHILD

A t 7:30 the next morning, Liv's hotel room door slowly opened as Kurt stepped quietly inside. Liv and Rose were playing on the floor with Rose's activity mat. Kurt gently placed down his carryon bag and then lay down on the floor, his eyes welling up with tears.

"Hi, sweet baby girl," he said. "I'm your daddy." Rose smiled and started moving her arms and legs rapidly. She then let out a loud squeal of delight. Kurt rolled over and put the baby on his chest. His voice cracked when he said, "I can't believe she's finally in my arms."

Liv filled Kurt in on the events of the trip so far. He laughed at the karaoke and dumpling stories. "I would have loved to have seen your mother's face when she saw the rest stop bathroom," he said. "So, we have to be at the visa office today at 10:30?"

"Yes. Mr. Hong will be here at 10:00 to pick us up."

The hotel phone rang just then and Liv got up to answer it. She listened and said, "Are you sure? Do we really have to meet them?

Okay, Susan, I understand. We'll see you at the visa office and then we can all go over together. Thanks for the call. See you soon."

"What was that all about?" asked Kurt after Liv hung up.

"Well, you're never going to believe this. After we're finished at the visa office, Susan, the adoption counselor, is going to take us to a coffee shop to meet Rose's birth mother and also her great-grandmother."

"All right," said Kurt. "We both knew going into this that it was the birth mother's right to meet us if she chose to."

"I know," said Liv. "It's just that I've been here now for almost two weeks, so at this point, I never thought it was going to happen."

"Well, Sweetheart, I don't know what to tell you except it looks like it's definitely happening," said Kurt, rising off the floor and handing Liv the baby. "I'm going to jump into the shower and change real quick before we have to leave for the visa appointment. And, Liv, please don't worry so much. Let's just get through today so we can finally take Rose home."

"Okay," said Liv. "You're right."

At ten o'clock, they were in Mr. Hong's minivan with Susan, heading over to the visa office. In less than an hour, Rose's visa was approved. *What a relief,* Liv thought. Liv told Kurt to go on ahead. "I'll meet you at the minivan. I need to use the restroom real quick."

Liv went into the restroom and stared into the mirror. "Come on, Olivia Whittaker, you can do this!" But no amount of self-encouragement could get her past the anxiety she felt about meeting Rose's birth mother. All of a sudden, the room began to spin. She thought for a moment that she might throw up. Liv splashed some cold water on her face and tried to pull herself together. Finally, she walked out of the restroom and met the others at the minivan.

"Is everything okay?" Susan asked.

"I'm fine. Just a little nervous."

"Don't worry. I'm sure she's nervous as well. And between you and me, I think this is her grandmother's doing."

Ten minutes later, they pulled up in front of the coffee shop. Susan led the way to the back of the restaurant where a young girl sat at a table wearing a pink Minnie Mouse T-shirt, pink barrettes, and jeans. She was only fourteen years old. Her grandmother had on a denim jacket with matching jeans. Liv guessed she was about forty-five. Susan introduced everyone and translated for the group. The grandmother told them that it had taken over four hours by train to get to Taipei due to the fact that they lived in a very remote area of Taiwan and were farmers by trade.

The grandmother went on to explain that the birth mother's parents had both been killed in a scooter accident several years ago, here in Taipei. She also made it very clear that the birth mother had hidden her pregnancy from her for seven months because she knew it would have brought shame to the family. She had met the birth father online in a chat room and only met him once in person. When she tried to locate him to tell him about her pregnancy, she was shocked to find out that he had provided her with false information about where he lived and attended school. Because of the birth mother's young age and the family's financial struggles, she had no choice but to put the baby up for adoption. *Wow*, Liv thought. *This girl is not a day older than William.*

Liv asked the birth mother if she would like to hold the baby. She nodded and hesitantly reached out for Rose. Liv placed the baby on her lap. Rose immediately started crying. Liv was shocked Rose hadn't cried once in the last ten days. Liv decided it was because the young girl didn't know how to hold the baby properly. It was essentially a child holding a child. The girl quickly handed Rose back to Liv.

Susan asked if anyone had any further questions. The birth mother explained she had a couple of favors to ask Kurt and Liv. Susan translated. "First of all, please don't spoil her."

Liv and Kurt looked at each other and both laughed. "We'll try," said Kurt, "but you don't know my wife."

"Secondly, once a year, can you please send me pictures of her through the adoption agency?"

"Of course," Liv replied. After that, they all stood up and Susan took several group photos, and then they all hugged and said their goodbyes. When everyone got back into the minivan, Liv felt an enormous sense of relief. And at the end of the day, she was very glad that they had all met. She also knew one day it might be important for Rose to see the photos and have the full story of her adoption.

Four days later, Liv, Rose, and her mother were sitting in the China Airlines lounge at the Taipei airport. As expected, after Rose's visa was issued, Kurt was on the first plane out the following morning heading back to the US. Liv couldn't believe that he had gotten on the plane. Liv had only been with Rose for two weeks now but it would have taken an army to pry her daughter away from her. *That man's morals are all screwed up.*

Liv's mother interrupted her thoughts. "Liv, do you want anything from the buffet?"

"No, Mom. I'm fine." Her mother returned with a glass of Chardonnay, a plate of steamed pork dumplings, pad Thai noodles, and a bowl of wonton soup.

"Mother, I honestly cannot believe you!" said Liv. "We've been in Taiwan for two weeks and you have refused to try any Asian food. We are now within hours of departing this country and you decide to have yourself an Asian feast."

Liv's mom laughed as she took a big bite out of one of the dumplings. "Liv, these are fantastic. You should really go get some."

Liv rolled her eyes and laughed. "Mother, it's time for us to go home." Liv's mom raised her wine glass and said, "I'll drink to that! Cheers, Baby Rose, we're taking you home!"

CHAPTER 52

ROSE'S FIRST BIRTHDAY

July 17th, 2010. Liv, Kurt, Rose, and the boys were all at Liv's parents' house at the Jersey shore to celebrate Rose's first birthday. Liv had decided to stay at her parents' home for the month of July, and Kurt was driving up from Virginia on the weekends. That morning, Rose was busy splashing around in her new baby pool wearing a pink ballerina bathing suit with a crown that read, "My First Birthday." Joe Leone's catering team was busy setting up for the party, but Liv had insisted on making Rose's first birthday cake herself.

Inside, the house was decorated with pink and white hydrangeas. And outside, clusters of balloons had been placed all around the deck and were being tossed around by the sea breeze. Liv had also arranged for a mimosa station to be set up along with two open bars. They were expecting over seventy-five people to come to the house that day to celebrate little Rose's first birthday.

But unfortunately, Liv wasn't feeling very well on her daughter's big day. Ever since May, she'd been dealing with a multitude of health issues, including fainting twice at the gym. Her primary doctor had run tests for diabetes and leukemia, both of which came back negative. Liv also was experiencing severe chest pains, along with horrible headaches, vomiting, diarrhea, extreme sweating, blurred vision, and she was even having difficulty walking.

Her doctor thought maybe she was suffering from panic attacks due to the stress of Kurt's absence and Rose's long adoption process. But her mother, on the other hand, thought that was complete nonsense. She told the doctor, "My daughter doesn't have an anxious bone in her body." To Liv, she said, "When doctors can't come up with a medical diagnosis for you, they just assume you're crazy."

But Liv did feel crazy. She had waited so long for her daughter's arrival and now she felt ill almost every day. She was forced to give up her morning exercise route and most of her other daily activities. She also had no choice but to hire a full-time nanny to help with Rose. Cora, Rose's new nanny, was originally from Haiti. Her family had come to the US when she was just three, but her mother had passed away when she was only fifteen. The oldest of six children, Cora had a lot of experience caring for children. She was wonderful with Rose, but Liv felt like a failure as a mother. She didn't want Cora's help; she just wanted to feel like herself again.

After months of appointments with local doctors, Liv had finally decided to go up to the Mayo Clinic in Jacksonville. She was hopeful that the doctors at Mayo could shed some light on her medical issues. But prior to her appointment in September, she was advised that she would have to wear a cardio monitor for the month of August to rule out any heart problems.

Liv was finishing getting dressed when Kurt walked into the bedroom. "Liv, the party looks fantastic," he said.

"Thanks. I just hope I didn't forget anything."

"Don't worry. It's going to be the perfect day, and we really did luck out with the weather. Seventy-five degrees and not a cloud in the sky," said Kurt. "So, how are you feeling?"

"Not so great. This is a lot. I think I might have done too much this week getting everything ready for the party."

"Liv, you definitely did too much. The doctors at Mayo told you not to overdo it until they can make a proper diagnosis."

"I know. But it's Rose's first birthday and the whole family is coming."

"That's my wife, always the perfectionist." He walked over and kissed her. "Now, Liv, please stop worrying. The party looks great, and you look beautiful as always." Kurt looked down at his watch. "Did you know it's almost noon? I think we'd better get outside to greet our guests."

"Kurt, you go on ahead. I just need a couple more minutes to finish getting ready, okay?"

"Sure. Take your time. I'll go check on Rose."

As soon as Kurt left the room, Liv sat on the end of her bed and prayed. *Dear God, thank you for bringing us all together to celebrate Rose's first birthday. Thank you for my amazing family and for my loving husband. Dear God, please help the doctors at Mayo find the answers that I am so desperately searching for. I just want to feel like myself again. Amen.*

CHAPTER 53

"GODDAMN IT!"

September 17th, 2010. Liv had been admitted to the Mayo Clinic as an outpatient for a little over two weeks now. After wearing the cardio monitor for a month as directed, the doctors had determined that there was a problem with her heart. She was diagnosed with sinus tachycardia. But that still didn't explain all of the other symptoms she was experiencing. Because of this, the doctors had decided to run more tests.

Liv, her mom, Rose, and Cora had been staying at the Ponte Vedra Inn during her outpatient stay. Kurt had flown in that morning for the weekend and would be leaving on Tuesday. He walked into the hotel room, dropped his carryon bag, and sat down on Liv's bed. He took her hand and asked, "Where is everyone?"

"Oh, they're all at the pool," said Liv.

"So on Monday, you're scheduled for the tilt table test."

"That's the plan."

Kurt got up and began to pace the room. "Liv, this is just so damn frustrating. Why the fuck can't they just figure out what the hell is wrong with you? I mean, Liv, our entire lives have been turned upside down. You're up here with Rose, Ms. Dee is down in Palm Beach with the boys, and I'm in DC. Liv, we need to get our normal lives back. And, as you know, I really shouldn't be missing all this work!"

Liv propped herself up on her pillows. "Kurt, let me ask you a question," she said. "Do you think I've been having fun these last few months? For God's sake, I've been treated like a goddamn guinea pig and the doctors still don't have a clue as to what is wrong with me. Let's face it, at this point I'm basically bedridden and I need assistance with every aspect of my life. Goddamn it, Kurt, sometimes you act like I'm doing all of this on purpose!"

She began to cry hysterically. Kurt went over to the bed and held her in his arms. "I'm sorry, I yelled, Liv. I just want my wife back and our kids need their mother."

"Believe me, no one wants to get to the bottom of my illness more than I do. I've literally been living in hell."

"I know, Liv. Well, we're at one of the best hospitals in the country with some of the best doctors. So hopefully, by the end of this week, we'll have all of the answers that we've been looking for."

"I pray you're right," said Liv, as she rolled over on her side and stared out the window, grateful that she could see and hear the ocean. She closed her eyes and thought, *Dear God, please help me. Please. I don't know how much more of this I can take.*

CHAPTER 54

THE TILT TABLE TEST

Monday morning, 7:00 a.m. Liv was admitted into the Mayo Clinic hospital for the tilt table test. The test involved a table that Liv would lie down on and then she would be raised upwards into a standing position. The idea was to see how her blood pressure and heart rate would respond when she went from a lying to a standing position.

Liv anxiously waited in her hospital room with Kurt and her mother by her side. She hadn't been allowed to eat or drink anything that day. At 12:30, a nurse entered the room with a wheelchair.

"Good afternoon, Mrs. Donovan. So, before I take you down for the test," she said, "I need to take your vitals and put an IV into your arm." *Great*, Liv thought. *More needles*. Over the last few months she had begun to feel like a pincushion.

"Okay, looks good," said the nurse after inserting the IV.

"I want to go with my wife if that's okay," said Kurt.

"Yes, Mr. Donovan, that's fine. You'll be permitted into the testing room, but once the test begins, you'll have to step outside.

There's an observation window in the room so you'll be able to see your wife for the duration of the test."

"Okay," said Kurt, putting his hands on Liv's shoulders. "Mom, do you also want to come?"

"Oh no, I'm fine here," Liv's mom said. "I've seen her go through enough of these tests over the last few months." Then she walked over to Liv, gave her a hug, squeezed her hand, and kissed her on the forehead.

"All right, let's go. The doctors are waiting for you," said the nurse.

When Liv arrived at the testing room, the electrocardiologist instructed her to lie down on the table.

"That looks good, Mrs. Donovan. We're going to strap you onto the table and then place EKG electrodes on your body to monitor your heart rate. Next, I'm going to slide the blood pressure cuff onto your left arm. It will take your blood pressure throughout the test. Alright, I think we're ready to proceed. I'm going to put a little medicine in your IV to get you started. Mr. Donovan, you'll need to step outside now so we can begin the test."

Kurt grabbed Liv's hands and kissed her on the cheek. "Don't worry, sweetheart, you'll be fine," he said. "And I'll be right outside. I love you."

Liv nodded.

"Okay, Mrs. Donovan," said the doctor, "we're going to raise the table to the upright position." Once she was upright, a platform was raised under Liv's feet putting her into a standing position. "We are going to remove the platform that you're standing on. On the count of three. Ready? One, two, three," said the doctor.

All Liv remembered was the floor dropping out from under her. She saw a bright light flash in front of her eyes and then everything went black. The next thing she knew she was being wheeled back to her room on a stretcher. She was covered in sweat and shaking profusely. Kurt was holding her hand. She looked up at him.

"What happened?"

"You failed the test sweetheart, but they now know what's wrong with you."

"They do?" Liv started to cry uncontrollably. *Thank God*, she thought. *Maybe this nightmare can finally be over.*

CHAPTER 55

"MRS. DONOVAN, YOU HAVE POTS"

After the tilt table test, as a precaution, Liv's cardiologist had decided to keep her overnight in the hospital for observation. Early the next morning, her team of doctors entered the room.

"Good morning, Mrs. Donovan," said Dr. Peng, Liv's head doctor at Mayo. "As you know, for the last few weeks, I have assembled a medical team to evaluate you, run tests, and meet as a group to come up with a proper diagnosis for your condition. Following your tilt table test yesterday, we reviewed your cardio monitor results and the other tests that were performed here at the Mayo Clinic. And at this point in time, Mrs. Donovan, we are all in agreement. You have a very rare condition called postural orthostatic tachycardia syndrome, also known as POTS. Basically, this condition affects patients when they go from the lying to standing position. There is an abnormally large increase in their heart rate which causes a multitude of symptoms including lightheadedness

213

and fainting. We're going to send you home with some new medications to try and a list of daily exercises. We do believe, in one to two months, we can get your daily symptoms under control and you can resume all of your normal activities."

Liv felt the warm tears run down her face. She looked over at her mom and Kurt, and then back to Dr. Peng.

"I'm going to be okay?"

"Oh yes, Mrs. Donovan, you're going to be just fine."

"Thank you," said Liv. "Thank you all so very much."

Kurt shook hands with all of the doctors and thanked each one as they filed out of the room. Liv's mom gave her a big hug.

"My little girl is going to be okay," she said. "Thank God."

Kurt sat down on Liv's bed and held her in his arms. "Thank God is right," he said. "Now we just need to get you home and better. Mom, let's go tell the nurses Liv is being discharged so we can head back to the hotel."

"Okay, and I'll go pull the car around while you're signing the discharge papers," Liv's mom said.

After they both left the room, Liv looked up at the ceiling and whispered, "Thank you, God. This nightmare is finally over and I get to go home to my babies."

CHAPTER 56

LIV'S NIGHTMARE HAD NOT ENDED

January 2011. Unfortunately for Liv, her nightmare had not ended. She was grateful for the diagnosis, but she hadn't gotten any better since she had returned home from Mayo. The doctors kept prescribing her medication after medication but each time she tried one, she ended up in the emergency room with an allergic reaction. At this point, she had tried over twenty-five different drugs, and each one had landed her in the hospital.

The daily exercises that Mayo recommended weren't helping either. The doctors wanted Liv to swim laps in order to build up her leg strength. The swimming was fine, but every time she got out of the pool, she fainted. Because she was still fainting on a regular basis, it wasn't safe for her to be left alone. She was also forced to move into the downstairs guest bedroom because the staircase was now off limits. Her mother, Ms. Dee, Cora, and the boys were taking turns caring for Liv.

For Liv, every day was the same routine. Cora and Rose would bring Liv breakfast in bed. After breakfast, Cora would help her shower and get dressed for the day. Liv always insisted on putting on her makeup, blow drying her hair, and dressing nicely each day. Liv felt that it was important that she looked good for when the boys returned home from school. Every day at 3:00, Cora would help her to the kitchen table. From there, Liv would instruct Cora on what ingredients to bring to her so she could assemble that night's dinner. Ms. Dee would set the table and help look after Rose. Each evening at six, Liv, Rose, and the boys would sit at the dining room table for their family dinner. After dinner, the boys would clean up and put Rose down for the night while Ms. Dee helped Liv get ready for bed.

January 18th, 11:00 a.m. Liv's mom came into her dark bedroom. "Liv, Cora said you didn't want breakfast today and you refused to get out of bed. What's going on?"

"Mom," said Liv, "Let's face it, this is no way to live. I've been trying so hard, but what kind of life is this, anyways? I lie here day after day and watch my children run and play in the backyard out of my bedroom window. Mom, I can't even take care of myself or my children. If I'm being completely honest, I truly believe that they would all be better off without me." Liv had a blank stare on her face. "I'm sorry, Mom, I just don't want to live anymore," she continued. "Not like this, anyway."

Liv's mother said nothing. She turned around and walked out of the room. When she returned, she was holding a professional portrait of Rose, William, Austin, and Jeffrey. She carefully laid it on Liv's lap.

"Olivia, you need to fight for them, if not for yourself, for your children," she said. "I'm telling you, Olivia, you can't give up."

Liv began to cry. "That's not fair, Mom."

"Liv, we're going to figure this out. I promise you."

Liv looked down at the photo. She loved her children more than anything.

"Liv," her mother continued, "your sister has been doing a lot of research on POTS and she found a specialist in Toledo, Ohio. I really think you should go see him. I brought you some of the articles that he's written." Liv's mom went over to her purse, pulled out the articles, and handed them to her.

Liv stared at the doctor's picture and wondered if he could really help her.

"Liv, let's call his office and try to make an appointment."

"Mom, I really don't see how you can expect me to travel all the way to Toledo, Ohio when I can hardly get out of bed."

"Liv, we'll worry about getting you there after you schedule an appointment."

"Okay, Mom," said Liv. "Whatever you say. Hand me my phone and I'll call." Liv's hands were sweating as she dialed the number.

"Thank you for calling the University of Toledo Cardiovascular Center," said the voice on the other end. "This is Carol. How can I help you today?"

"Well, I was hoping to make an appointment with Dr. Grubb," said Liv.

"Okay, sweetie. And what would you be coming to see Dr. Grubb for?"

"I was diagnosed with POTS at the Mayo Clinic in Jacksonville."

"I see. Did they perform the tilt table test on you?"

"Oh, yes, it was awful."

"Well, here's the situation with Dr Grubb. There's a four-year waiting list to see him." *Oh, God,* thought Liv. "But please don't let that deter you, dear. Call Mayo and have them fax your medical records directly over to me. Dr. Grubb goes through each file himself and the patients he feels truly do have POTS get moved to the top of the list and it sounds like you definitely do. Odds are you'll probably get a call from us within six months to a year."

Six months to a year, Liv thought. "Carol, I have four kids. I really need this appointment."

"Olivia, I understand. So, call Mayo as soon as we hang up and send me your records. And I promise to do all I can for you."

"Okay, Carol, I'll get them over to you today, and thank you." Liv hung up and told her mom what Carol had said.

"All right," said her mom, "see, now, there's hope. An hour ago, there was none. Now let's give Mayo a call and have your records sent. And then we pray."

CHAPTER 57

"HOLY TOLEDO. HERE I COME!"

May 5th, 2011. Liv was sitting at the kitchen table assembling a lasagna for dinner when Ms. Dee walked into the kitchen with the cordless phone. "The phone for you, Ms. Olivia," she whispered.

Liv answered to find Carol, the receptionist from Dr. Grubb's office, on the other end.

"Good afternoon, Mrs. Donovan, I have some good news for you today."

"You do, Carol? What is it?" asked Liv.

"Dr. Grubb has an opening on May 15th at 8:30 a.m."

"Wow, Carol, that *is* good news. But I think there may be a problem. I have to be honest with you. I don't know how I would get there. I can hardly walk at this point."

"I realize traveling here is going to be very difficult for you, but do you really want to give up this appointment?"

"No. Carol, I've read all about Dr. Grubb and I know if there is one person in this world that can help me, it's him! Let me speak to my family. And I know we'll figure something out. And don't worry. I'll definitely be there on May 15th."

"Okay, great. We'll see you then, Mrs. Donovan," said Carol.

"Ms. Olivia, what was that all about?" asked Ms. Dee after Liv had hung up.

"Well, Dr. Grubb, the doctor in Toledo, Ohio has an appointment for me in a couple of weeks."

"He does? Ms. Olivia, it's a miracle! This is what we've all been praying for. I knew God would answer our prayers."

"Ms. Dee, calm down. I don't even know how I'm going to get there."

"Ms. Olivia, where there's a will there's a way. Now, you better call your mama and tell her the good news. She's been worried sick about you."

"Yes, you're right." Liv called her mom and told her everything.

"Liv, this is great news! I'm so happy for you."

"But, Mom, how will I get there? It's so far away."

"Olivia, there are trains, planes, and if we have to drive you there, we'll do it. Don't worry. I give you my word—we will get you to that appointment!"

"Okay, Mom. "You're right. We'll figure it out." Liv hung up the phone and glanced over at Ms. Dee. "Well Ms. Dee, holy Toledo here I come!"

"Now that's the spirit, Ms. Olivia! Praise the Lord. She's going to Toledo!"

CHAPTER 58

THE ANGEL IN THE WHITE COAT

May 15th, 2011, 8:30 a.m., The University of Toledo Vascular Health Center. By the grace of God and the generosity of her family, Liv had made it to Toledo, Ohio. The Gallagher family had joined forces and decided to charter Liv a private plane to get her there and back safely. Kurt had taken a week off from his training to help Liv prepare for the trip and go along with her.

Liv, Kurt, and her mom were in Dr. Grubb's waiting room when her name was called.

"Okay," said Kurt. "Here we go." He wheeled Liv through the double doors into the examining room where the nurse asked Liv a battery of questions and took her vitals.

"Okay, I think that about does it," the nurse said. "Dr. Grubb will be in shortly."

Liv's hands were sweating. *He has to be able to help me*, she thought.

Before long, the examination door opened. "Good morning. I'm Dr. Grubb." Liv shook his hand. His hand was soft and he had a warm, gentle smile. "Thanks for coming all this way to see me."

221

"You're my last chance," Liv blurted out.

"Believe me, Olivia, I promise to do everything I can to help you," said Dr. Grubb, "so let's get to know each other a little better." He sat down at the computer and pulled up a number of graphs, charts, and diagrams to help better explain to Liv what her body was experiencing. Kurt had brought his laptop along and was taking notes throughout the course of the meeting.

"Well, Liv, you definitely have POTS," Dr. Grubb explained, "but many doctors aren't aware that there are thirty-eight different kinds of POTS. The Mayo Clinic diagnosed you with the most common form, but I have a feeling you have one of the rarer forms, if not the rarest. So what I would like to do is run a few more tests this morning. After that, you can go have lunch and then we'll all meet back here around three o'clock to discuss the test results. Okay?"

"Sure," said Liv.

"All right. I'm going to have you head on over to the lab and let them do their work and then go have a nice lunch."

The lab took eight tubes of blood and a urine sample.

Over lunch they all discussed the morning meeting. "I think, hands down, he's the smartest man I've ever met," said Kurt.

"I agree," said Liv's mom. "And to think he's dedicated his entire life to this disorder. We are finally at the right spot. Don't you agree, Olivia?"

"Yes, Mom. I can hardly put it into words, but he understands exactly what I've been going through these last few years. Kurt, can we please get the check? I don't want us to be late for our afternoon appointment."

Back in the examining room, they all eagerly awaited the lab results. Dr. Grubb soon came in and sat back down at the computer.

"Well," he said, "let's have a look. Yes. Just as I had suspected." Looking up from his computer he said, "Olivia, you have hyperadrenic POTS. It's the rarest form. You also have mast cell disorder. Your body is producing over a thousand times more histamine than the average person. And last but not least, you also have cyp2d6 inhibitors, which is why you are having such a hard time tolerating medications. The first thing I want to do is get you on a low sodium, high-protein diet. Next, you'll need to take a histamine blocker to control the mast cell. Now, Olivia, I have to be honest with you, because of your drug intolerance, you're going to have to work much harder than most of my other patients in order to get better."

"But she *is* going to get better, right, Dr. Grubb?" Liv's mother interrupted.

"I promise to get you seventy percent better from where you are right now," said Dr. Grubb.

"Dr. Grubb, I have a question."

"What is it, Olivia?" Dr. Grubb asked.

"Can I please go to Italy?" Liv asked. "My son William is graduating from high school in a few years and his dream graduation gift is a family trip to Italy."

Dr. Grubbs smiled. "I see. Well, let's get you walking again first. Then we can discuss Italy."

They all smiled. "Okay," said Liv.

"Now," said Dr. Grubb, "if I could please speak to my new favorite patient in private." Kurt and Liv's mom left the room and Dr. Grubb pulled up a chair and took Liv's hand. "So, tell me Olivia, how are you *really* doing?" he said.

Liv's eyes filled with tears. She looked deeply into Dr. Grubb's crystal blue eyes and said, "Every day is like living in my own private hell. I feel like a burden to my family. I don't have very many friends left because no one understands my illness. These last few years have been very depressing for me and unbelievably hard on my family."

"You're very pretty, Olivia," said Dr. Grubb, "so people don't see you as being ill or the unbearable pain that you have been living with. But don't worry, I understand how you're feeling. POTS is an incredibly isolating illness."

"Yes, it's terribly lonely," Liv replied.

"Believe me, I know," said Dr. Grubb. "So, all I'm going to ask of you is to do exactly as I instruct. You are quite literally going to have to retrain your body to learn how to walk again, and it's not going to be an easy road. But I know you can do it."

At that very moment, for the first time, Liv felt hope. "I give you my word. I promise to follow your instructions to the letter. All I want is my life back."

"Okay, so let's get you better, beautiful."

"I'm so grateful I got this opportunity to have met you today," said Liv.

"Me, too. Have a safe flight home and I'll be in touch this week with a personalized plan to get you feeling better."

"Thank you," said Liv. As Dr. Grubb shut the door, Liv closed her eyes. *Wow,* she thought. *He's going to get me better. I just know it. I finally found my angel in a white coat. Thank you, God.*

224

CHAPTER 59

"MAY YOU GO FROM STRENGTH TO STRENGTH"

November 5, 2011. Liv and Kurt had just returned home from Liv's second appointment with Dr. Grubb. Liv had never worked so hard in all of her life at anything. It was a slow process, but she was finally starting to get better.

After some trial and error, Dr. Grubb found a drug that helped constrict the veins in Liv's legs to help get the blood to her heart in a more timely manner. And because of this, she hadn't fainted once in over six months.

The final piece to Liv's recovery was that she had to start walking again on her own. At first, she was using Rose's high chair on wheels to assist her, but eventually, she started walking on her own a little at a time. One day, she'd gone to the front door and stared out at their mailbox at the end of the driveway. *Okay*, she thought. *Let's go get the mail.* Carefully and very slowly, she started walking across the cobblestone driveway toward the mailbox.

Ms. Dee came running out of the house after her. "Ms. Olivia, what are you doing?!"

"Ms. Dee, I'm going to get the mail today," Liv declared.

"You don't need to do that," said Ms. Dee. "Let me help you back into the house."

"No, Ms. Dee, I can do this. It's time."

"Okay, Ms. Olivia, whatever you say," said Ms. Dee, "but I'm going to be standing here the whole time just in case."

It took Liv forty-five minutes to walk to her mailbox and back to the house, but she did it. And thankfully, she didn't fall or faint. Liv felt as though she'd climbed a mountain that day.

So, for the next week, she walked to her mailbox, the following week to her neighbor's, and so on. Walking the mailboxes, her new high-protein diet, the medications, acupuncture, and therapy were all slowly giving Liv her life back. And there had been another big factor in her road to recovery. Kurt had done the unthinkable. He'd decided to quit the CIA training program. Dr. Grubb had made a big impression on him and he finally realized his place was at home by his wife's side.

At first, Liv was concerned that Kurt was going to resent her down the road, but he'd explained that the more he learned about the position the CIA had in mind for him, the more he realized it just wasn't a good fit for their family. The CIA wanted Kurt and the family to move to Dubai that coming summer. Kurt couldn't see how that would be possible. Liv was just starting to get better. William and Austin were excelling in high school. Jeffrey was in that fragile, awkward, middle-school age, and Liv's whole family had fallen in love with Baby Rose.

No. At the end of the day, Kurt had decided to put his family first. He'd gone back to running Eagle Armor and his Palm Beach sports car dealership. Liv was happy and relieved to have her husband back home. She was also grateful that he had made the decision to leave the CIA on his own. There was no doubt that their marriage had been strained by his absence and her illness, but Liv finally felt that they were both on the same page.

On this November day, Liv was in the kitchen preparing a roasted chicken for dinner when Kurt walked in with a package. He kissed her and handed her the package.

"This was out on the front porch," he said. "It's addressed to you." Liv carefully opened the box. Inside was a book written by Dr. Grubb, *The Calling*, a series of short stories. There was also a collection of poems, along with some artwork.

"Wow, Kurt," said Liv, "look at all of this. I can't believe he sent this to me." Liv opened the book and on the inside cover, it read,

For Olivia. May you go from strength to strength.

—Blair Grubb

Tears rolled down her face. She knew at that moment she had not only been given a second chance at her life, but also a second chance with her marriage.

CHAPTER 60

THE OLIVIA DONOVAN FOUNDATION FOR POTS RESEARCH

June 5th, 2013. William's high school graduation day. As Liv studied the graduation program waiting for the ceremony to begin, she looked around at all of her family and friends who were in attendance and thought back over the last two years. So much had happened.

Kurt was now producing his own line of military products. Austin received a full golf scholarship and was almost done with his freshman year at Duke University. William was following in Austin's footsteps and would be attending Duke in the fall. He had received a lacrosse scholarship and couldn't wait to start college. Jeffrey had just finished up his freshman year of high school. He was on the honor roll all year and continued to be a star on the basketball court. Baby Rose wasn't such a baby anymore. She was attending preschool at Palm Beach Country Day.

Liv was extremely proud of all of her children and of her family. They had weathered the storm of her illness and she was finally doing so much better. She was now walking an hour a day, seven days a week. She and Kurt were back to their weekly date nights. And the family was traveling once again. Last summer, they all went back to the Jersey Shore for the first time in two years, and had also returned to Sea Island for the 4th of July. Traveling was not easy for Liv, but she was staying well-hydrated and was using a wheelchair, as directed by Dr. Grubb. She had also been given the green light by Dr. Grubb to travel to Italy that summer. For William's graduation trip, the family was going to Rome, Portofino, and Florence. It was truly a dream come true for Liv and the entire family, but Liv knew without the help and kindness of Dr. Grubb, she wouldn't be where she was today.

During her last visit with him, she had taken his hand and, with tears in her eyes, had said, "How can I possibly thank you for giving me my life back?"

"Olivia, you worked very hard to get where you are today," said Dr. Grubb. "You, Olivia, are a fighter."

"Dr. Grubb, Kurt and I have been discussing what we could possibly do to show you our appreciation. Thanking you just isn't enough. So the question is, what can we do?"

"Well, Olivia, as you know, there are just a handful of doctors in the US who specialize in POTS. The bottom line is we need more doctors, research money, and we also need to raise awareness about this disorder. My team here at the Toledo Vascular Center is working on developing a blood test to diagnose patients with POTS more rapidly in order to get them on the road to recovery faster. But this is a very costly endeavor."

Liv smiled and looked into Dr. Grubb's crystal clear blue eyes. "I have an idea. What if I start a charity organization and, once a year, I'll have a big fundraiser to help raise research money and awareness for POTS? I've never done anything like this before, but I'm willing to give it a try."

"That would be wonderful, Olivia. Every bit helps and I truly do believe you are a great inspiration to so many POTS patients all around the world."

"I'll start working on it next week!"

And Liv had done just that. She had started her own charity organization called the Olivia Donovan Foundation for POTS Research. She had a Facebook page, website, and had done several email blasts to help raise money and awareness. This had become Olivia's new passion.

As William walked across the stage and was handed his diploma, Liv began to cry tears of joy. Kurt put his arm around her and kissed her cheek. Olivia Donovan had truly gone from strength to strength.

CHAPTER 61

KURT APPARENTLY HAD NO PLANS TO GROW OLD GRACEFULLY

October 14th, 2014. Kurt and Liv had checked into the Four Seasons Hotel in Palm Beach for Liv's birthday weekend. Liv stepped out onto the balcony of their suite and stared out at the ocean, reflecting on the last few years. Austin and William were both doing great at Duke. Jeffrey was applying to colleges and was hoping to play basketball for the University of Georgia. And beautiful little Rose had just started kindergarten. Overall, Liv's children were thriving. Meanwhile, Liv's foundation for POTS research was also doing quite well, and she was very excited about the foundation's first charity golf event coming up that following summer.

The only real difficulty in Liv's life at the moment was Kurt. As Liv looked out at the ocean, she thought back to their family vacation to Sea Island this past July. Kurt had been acting very strangely for a few months prior to the trip. He was constantly on his laptop and phone. He was drinking a lot. Two bottles of red wine almost every night. And he was also hardly sleeping.

One afternoon at Sea Island, Liv had filled up the soaking tub to get all of the sand off of Rose after a long day at the beach. She then went to put Rose's swimsuit in the washing machine when she overheard Kurt on the phone in the living room.

"I told you, Roger, four million for a piece of my company is a bargain. I guarantee you're going to double your money within a year. Yes, I understand your concerns, but you have to trust me on this." At that point, Kurt looked up and saw Liv. "Roger, I have to go. I'll give you a call back tomorrow so we can go over the contract." He hung up and turned to Liv. "Liv, how long have you been standing there?"

"Kurt, what are you up to?"

"Well, as a matter of fact, I'm taking a four-million-dollar business loan from a very wealthy gentleman who lives out in Beverly Hills. That's what I'm up to."

"What? Why on earth would you do that?"

"Liv, I need more inventory. I can't bid on huge contracts if I can't fill the orders."

"But, Kurt, what's the rush? Your companies are all doing great. And in my opinion, I think you're trying to grow your businesses too fast. Just look at my family's company. It grew over generations. That's why it's still around today."

"You're cute, Liv. But you don't know the first thing about running a company."

"Well, I disagree. There are no shortcuts in life, Kurt. And another thing, you act like four million dollars is nothing. That's a hell of a lot of money. And why on earth would you want to give up a piece of your company? I'm telling you, Kurt, this is a huge mistake."

"Liv, I suggest you stick with what you're best at and leave running the businesses to me." As always, Liv knew there was no changing Kurt's mind. She also knew he was definitely going to take the loan.

Two months later, Kurt turned forty-five and he was more stressed out than ever. He was still drinking way too much and was staying up all hours of the night on the family's computer. He was overweight and hardly ever slept. He was also incredibly irritable and was never in a good mood. And on top of everything else, he was also having trouble in the bedroom. Their family doctor explained that this was common as a man got older and prescribed Viagra, but Kurt decided to flush the pills down the toilet. He apparently had no plans to grow old gracefully. He even decided to buy himself a Harley Davidson Fatboy motorcycle as a birthday present to himself. Liv started to think he was having some sort of mid-life crisis.

A few weeks after his birthday, Kurt was in the shower and his gym bag was opened on the bed. Liv went to move the bag and a small case fell out. She had never seen the case before, so she decided to open it. Inside were four prefilled syringes. *What on earth?* she thought. She took the case into the bathroom and confronted Kurt.

"Kurt, what the hell is this?"

"Liv, why are you going through my things?"

"Kurt, just answer the question."

"If you must know, Liv, I'm trying to lose weight. I want my Navy SEAL body back."

"So you've been injecting yourself with this shit? I honestly can't believe you! Kurt, tell me the truth. How long have you been doing this?"

"Just a month."

"Well, this needs to stop right now. This stuff can be dangerous."

"Liv, stop acting like my mother. I'm not going to stop and you're going to love the results."

"Kurt, I don't give a shit what you look like!"

Finally, after many arguments, Kurt promised to throw away the syringes and go back to just plain old diet and exercise.

Now, at the Four Seasons, Liv stepped back into their suite. Kurt had gone for a run on the beach and Liv decided to take a bubble bath before dinner. In the bedroom, her eyes fell upon Kurt's suitcase. Part of her thought she shouldn't, but her woman's intuition said she should. She opened up his suitcase and rummaged through it, finding what she hoped would not be there: the same case that she had found before. She unzipped it and, sure enough, found the same syringes.

Furious, Liv called for a cab, packed up her suitcase, and headed to the lobby. She decided to head home to spend her birthday with Rose and Jeffrey. From the back of the cab, she sent a text to Kurt: "Thanks for ruining my birthday. Liv."

CHAPTER 62

SECRETS BEHIND THE HEDGES

E aster, 2015. Liv was driving home after dropping William and Austin off at the airport. She was sad to see them leave after the long Easter weekend. The family had dyed Easter eggs, hosted a neighborhood egg toss, went to the beach, and attended Easter Sunday service. Overall, it had been a wonderful weekend.

From an outsider's perspective, everything looked the same in the Donovan's household. But inside, things had taken a turn for the worse. Much to Liv's frustration and disappointment, Kurt was still injecting himself four times a day. His mood swings had become unbearable to say the least. Every morning, he would send Liv a text message instructing her what to prepare for his dinner. If he walked in the door and his Perrier and correct meal was not on the table, he would go into a crazy rage. He still hardly ever slept, but when he did, it was in the guest room. He would come into their bedroom twice a week for sex. Liv hated every second of it but was afraid not to comply.

Kurt was also taking out his frustrations on Jeffrey. He told him his grades weren't good enough and his SAT scores were too low.

He criticized everything from his outward appearance to his table manners. The two began having explosive arguments that ended with Jeffrey locking himself in his room out of pure fear. On the flip side, Rose could do no wrong. Kurt was constantly buying her gifts and Liv was afraid that he was turning their lovely daughter into a spoiled brat. Kurt and Liv weren't agreeing on anything at this point. Kurt said Liv was spending too much money, he criticized her parenting skills constantly, and had even accused her of having multiple affairs. It was as if Liv was living with a complete stranger.

One day, Liv decided to ask Kurt if maybe they should try going to couples therapy to work through some of their differences. He told her she was the one with the problems, not him. She even often wondered if a trial separation might be for the best, but she was too afraid to bring it up to him. No, Liv had decided to just grin and bear it. They had been through so much over the last nineteen years and she held firm in the belief that, somehow, they would make it through this terrible time.

Liv turned down Seaspray Avenue, her all-American street lined with beautiful, Mediterranean-style homes with perfectly manicured lawns all surrounded by fifteen-foot hedges. She put her car in park at the end of her driveway and stared at the house, not wanting to go in. Her home was every girl's dream from the outside, but on the inside, she was trapped, living with a man and in a marriage that was unrecognizable to her. She slowly got out of her car and looked up at the night sky, wondering how many other families on her street were hiding their family secrets behind the hedges.

CHAPTER 63

HAPPY ANNIVERSARY

June 14th, 2015. Today was Liv and Kurt's twenty-first wedding anniversary. Even though nothing had changed between them over the last few months, Kurt had insisted on celebrating their anniversary at The Breakers Hotel. Although Liv had her reservations about going, she finally gave in and agreed to the overnight trip.

As Liv walked into the kitchen to make her morning coffee, she noticed a card that was propped up on the coffeemaker that read "Happy Anniversary, Liv." She sat down with her coffee at the kitchen table and slowly slid the card out of the envelope. On the front, the card read, "Happy Anniversary." Inside, there was a handwritten note from Kurt.

Dear Liv,

I just want to thank you for being the best wife and mother over the last twenty-one years. I also wanted to thank you for loving me unconditionally and for showing me the true meaning of family. And last but not least, I want to apologize for this last year. I know things have been extremely difficult between us but I really want to put all of that behind us. You truly are my best friend and I give you my solemn promise that things will be different between us after today. So tonight, let's celebrate all of the great times that we have shared together over the years. I love you with all my heart.

Yours always and forever,

Kurt XO

Liv closed the card and thought, *Maybe if we both really try, we can still put our marriage back together.*

Later that morning, Liv and Kurt checked into The Breakers to begin their anniversary celebration. They had lunch by the pool and then spent the afternoon on the beach. Liv could tell Kurt was trying very hard to make this a special anniversary for the both of them. He had even surprised her by booking their same honeymoon suite and had also arranged for a private dinner in the ballroom where their wedding reception was held. That evening, when Liv walked into the ballroom for dinner, she was stunned. It was decorated exactly the same way as it had been twenty-one years prior.

"Kurt, my God, it's like stepping back in time!" On the table was a dozen red roses, a bottle of Rombauer Chardonnay, and a card that said, *It had to be you.* "Kurt, I can't believe you went to all of this trouble for me."

"Do you like it?"

"Are you kidding? I love it."

The waiter came over to the table, opened the Chardonnay, and handed Liv the dinner menu. On the top of the menu it read, *"Happy Anniversary Liv and Kurt."*

"Mrs. Donovan, your husband has selected the items on this evening's menu especially for you," the waiter said. Liv looked it over: First course: Oysters Rockefeller; Second course: Caesar salad; Third course: Chateaubriand with béarnaise sauce and mixed vegetables.

"It looks wonderful," Liv said.

"May I pour the wine?" asked the waiter.

"Yes," replied Kurt, "and we're also going to have a bottle of red, as well. The Caymus, 40th Anniversary, will be perfect with our main course."

"That's an excellent choice, sir," said the waiter. "I'll go down to the wine cellar and decant it right away for you, sir."

"Kurt, this is fabulous," said Liv. "I honestly don't know what to say."

"Liv, you have always been my princess. So tonight, please let me spoil you."

The waiter returned with the wine and placed a silver-domed dinner plate in the center of the table.

"The chef has prepared a little something special to start off your evening," he said. "May I?" Kurt nodded and the waiter removed the dome. On the plate rested a huge diamond ring in the shape of a scallop shell.

"What on earth?" said Liv. "Kurt, it can't be!" Liv carefully picked up the ring. In the center was a three-carat diamond and on the fans of the ring were smaller diamonds surrounded by rubies. Liv knew this ring well. She had admired it her whole life. Her great uncle, Adam, had given it to her great aunt, Fran, as an engagement ring. "How in the world did you get my mother to agree to give you this ring?"

"Well, as you know," said Kurt, "your mother is quite fond of that ring and she wasn't willing to part with it. So, I decided to have one made especially for you. If you look closely, yours has a canary diamond in the center, and it's also much bigger than your Aunt Fran's ring."

"Kurt, I don't know what to say. It's absolutely stunning," said Liv. "And I honestly can't believe you went through all of this trouble for me."

"I told you, Liv, tonight is a fresh start."

Over dinner, Liv and Kurt laughed, reminisced, and enjoyed their beautiful meal. After dinner, they danced to their wedding song, "It Had to Be You." As they were dancing, Liv looked into Kurt's eyes. He leaned down and whispered in her ear, "You know Liv, it has always been you from the first moment I saw you." Then he passionately kissed her. "What do you say we have dessert sent up to the room?"

"Good idea," Liv whispered back and then she kissed him again.

Up in their suite there was a trail of red rose petals and candles leading to the bed. Laid out on the bed was a sexy black lingerie outfit.

"Darling, I was hoping I might have *you* for dessert," said Kurt. "That is, if you'll let me."

Liv picked up the lingerie, tossed it over her shoulder, and headed into the bathroom. She slid on the black lace lingerie and smiled. She was excited to make love to her husband. She walked out of the bathroom and Kurt kissed her, picked her up, and laid her carefully on the bed. "I love making love to you," he said.

For the next few hours, they made love like they hadn't in years. They were hungry for each other and the passion between them was electric. Neither one could get enough.

As Liv fell asleep in her husband's arms, she felt safe and at peace once again. That night, she slept like an angel, hoping that they could stay this way forever.

CHAPTER 64

THE FAIRY TALE
WAS OFFICIALLY OVER

The next morning, Liv woke up feeling completely satisfied and blissful after her romantic evening with her husband. She rolled over to snuggle with Kurt, but he wasn't there. Presuming he was in the bathroom, she called out, "Kurt, do you want me to order breakfast from room service?" Hearing no reply, she put on her hotel robe and went into the bathroom, but, much to her surprise, Kurt wasn't there. She then noticed his shaving kit wasn't on the vanity and his suitcase was missing as well.

Maybe there was a problem at work, she thought. She grabbed her cell phone and dialed Kurt but it went straight to voicemail. She then tried his office, but the secretary said he wasn't in. It suddenly occurred to her that maybe something had happened to one of the kids. She hurried to get dressed, packed her suitcase, and called the front desk for a cab.

Twenty minutes later, the cab pulled into their driveway but there was no sign of Kurt's car. She opened the front door and called, "Kurt…Kurt, are you home?"

Ms. Dee came out from the kitchen. "Miss Olivia, you're home early. I wasn't expecting you until this evening. Is everything okay?"

"Oh, yes, Ms. Dee, I'm sure everything's fine," replied Liv. "But have you seen Kurt?"

"No, not since he left with you yesterday."

Just then the doorbell rang. Liv ran to the door. When she opened it, there stood a deliveryman holding a huge bouquet of flowers.

"Are you Olivia Donovan?" he said.

"Yes."

"Can you please sign right here for me?" Liv signed the paper. He then handed her an envelope and the flowers.

"What's this?" she asked, holding up the envelope.

"Olivia Donovan, you just got served," the man replied.

"Served? Served what?" asked Liv, but the man was already halfway up the driveway.

"Wait!" Liv said, chasing after him, waving the envelope. "What *is* this?"

The man stopped and said, "Listen, lady, I'm just doing my job."

Liv tore open the envelope. At the top of the court document, it read: "Dissolution of Marriage."

"Look," said Liv, "there has to be some sort of mistake."

"No mistake, ma'am. You're getting divorced."

"Divorced? No! This is crazy." But the man hopped into his car and drove off.

Liv ran back into the house.

"What is going on, Miss Olivia?" asked Ms. Dee.

"I'm not sure. Look." She handed Ms. Dee the paperwork.

"Mr. Kurt filed for divorce? Has he lost his mind? Oh my God, Miss Olivia. This has to be a mistake!"

Liv grabbed her cell to try to call Kurt again, but just as she did, the phone rang. It was William.

"Mom, are you okay?"

"William, we need to talk."

"Mom, I already know."

"What do you mean you already know?"

"Dad sent us all a text."

"William, what did it say?"

"'Divorcing Mom, Pops' He sent it about a half hour ago to me, Austin, and Jeffrey. Mom, what's going on?"

"William, I have no idea. We had a wonderful evening last night. I just don't understand. None of this makes any sense."

"Look, Mom, Austin and I are going to head to the airport to catch the next plane home."

"But what about summer school?"

"Mom, forget summer school, we're coming home."

"Okay. William, I love you."

"I love you, too."

Liv hung up the phone and told Ms. Dee what William had said. She then ran to the family computer. She logged into their bank accounts and saw to her horror that every account read zero. Joint account: zero. William's account: zero. Austin's account: zero. Jeffrey's account: zero. Rose's account: zero. Even her charity organization had been completely wiped out.

Liv screamed, "Oh, my God, he took all of our money!"

She immediately called her mother, breathlessly explaining everything.

"Liv, listen to me," her mother said, "try to calm down. You're going to have to call an attorney."

"Mom, I don't want to call an attorney."

"Olivia, you have no choice. He's taken all of your money and

God knows what else he's planned. Now, let me make some phone calls. I need to find you a really good attorney. I'll call you back shortly with some names."

Liv hung up the phone and just then all of the lights in the house went out. She called the electric company only to hear that the electricity had been turned off at Kurt's request.

"Well, sir, can I give you a credit card over the phone to get the electricity back on?" she asked the customer service representative. She read off the credit card's numbers only to be told her card had been declined. She tried two other cards and got the same result. Finally, Ms. Dee handed Liv her own credit card.

"Thanks," Liv whispered. And, thankfully, within the hour, the power was back on.

Liv's head was spinning. She had exactly thirty-eight dollars in her wallet. She tried calling Kurt again, but still no answer. Then she remembered. A few years ago, David Santoro had written her a letter. He had moved back to Florida and was living in Boca. He owned a chain of very successful restaurants in South Florida and was doing quite well. Liv ran upstairs to find his letter. After rummaging through her closet, she finally found it and reread it. At the end of the letter, David had written:

Liv, I wish things for us had turned out differently but I want you to know I will always love you. And if you ever need anything, I'm always here.

Love, David.

Then he had written his phone number. Liv grabbed her cell phone and dialed. On the third ring, he answered.

"David, it's Liv."

"Liv! Oh, my gosh, how are you, stranger?"

"Not so good," she replied and then she started to cry as she told him what had happened.

"Let me get this straight. That son of a bitch is leaving you? After taking you out to dinner, giving you a beautiful ring, and having sex with you all night? What a sick bastard!"

"Listen, David, I don't have any money. He took everything. David, I have four kids."

"Liv, try to calm down," said David. "I promise it's all going to be okay. Liv, you need to call an attorney."

Liv began to sob. "How could he do this to me and the kids?"

"I don't know," said David. "He's sick. But, listen, Liv, take the number of this attorney down. Her name is Abby Goldstein. She's one of the best. Call her and then call me back."

"Okay, I'll call her right after we hang up." Liv wrote down the number and then sat on the edge of her bed with her head in her hands, sobbing uncontrollably.

Ms. Dee walked in with a box of tissues.

"Don't worry, Miss Olivia. It's all going to be okay. You're a strong woman, and you mustn't forget that your children need you now more than ever. Oh, and by the way, it would seem that Mr. Kurt has also turned off the cable."

Liv started crying again. "I guess I really do need to call this attorney."

Ms. Dee handed her the phone and soon Liv was going over the events of the last twenty-four hours with Abby Goldstein.

"I just know there must be some kind of mistake," Liv said. "I mean, who plans a beautiful evening and just leaves their spouse like this?"

"Mrs. Donovan," said Abby Goldstein, "I don't know quite how to tell you this, but what just happened to you is called the goodbye dinner. It means he's been planning to leave for months, maybe even a year or more."

Liv felt as if she going to vomit.

"Be at my office tomorrow morning at 9:00 a.m.," Abby continued. "And don't forget to bring all of your jewelry."

"My jewelry? Why?"

"A lot of times, jewelry is not considered a gift. I'll have to keep it in my office safe until this mess is all sorted out. I'll see you tomorrow."

A goodbye dinner, thought Liv. *Planning this for months or years. I thought we could make it through anything. I thought we were a family.*

Just then, Liv got a text message: *Liv, I just couldn't do it anymore. The marriage, the house, the kids. Take care of yourself, Kurt.*

She threw her phone against the wall and sobbed some more. The fairy tale was officially over!

Epilogue

Later that night, Liv was curled up in her bed in the fetal position, hugging her pillow and crying. William slowly cracked her bedroom door open.

"Mom, are you awake? I'm home." Liv sat up and William gave his mother a warm hug and then sat on her bed.

"William, I'm so glad you're home. I don't understand what your father is doing. How do you just decide all of a sudden that you don't want to be a husband and a father anymore after twenty-one years of marriage?"

"I don't know, Mom."

"William, I think I've been a pretty good wife and mother over the years. Now, I do realize my getting sick was rough on everyone, but we took vows and we made promises. Doesn't that mean anything? Okay, so he doesn't want to be married to me anymore, but after twenty-one years together, wouldn't you have the common decency to sit down and have a conversation with your wife? Why, William? Why did he do this? Not just to me, but to all of us?"

William hugged her again. "Mom, let's face it, Dad has been acting differently for quite some time now. And by the way, just so you know, I'm not a kid anymore. Mom, I've noticed his excessive drinking, his new tattoos, and Dad's obsession with country music concerts. It's all super weird. And I also know he's been sleeping in the guest room for a while now."

"William, do you think there's someone else?"

"To be honest with you, Mom, it really wouldn't surprise me."

"Well, William, I can tell you this. I've been faithful to that man for twenty-one years."

"Listen, Mom, I think you need to get some sleep."

"William, I really don't think that I can. I'm scared of what's going to happen to all of us."

"Don't worry, Mom. We're going to figure this all out. I'll stay here with you until you fall asleep."

"Okay," said Liv as she lay down.

William tucked his mother in and slept in a chair by her side all night.

The next morning, Liv was in Abby Goldstein's waiting room with her mother by her side. Mrs. Goldstein's secretary opened the office door and said, "Mrs. Donovan, if you'll please follow me, Mrs. Goldstein is ready for you."

Liv and her mother followed the secretary into the conference room where five people sat around a large conference table.

"Good morning, Mrs. Donovan. I'm Abby Goldstein and this is your legal team." Mrs. Goldstein introduced Liv to two paralegals and two forensic accountants. "First of all, I just want to start out by saying that everyone around this table is very sorry that this has happened to you and your family. We all know divorce is never easy."

"But here's the thing," said Liv. "I don't want to get divorced. I think a trial separation would be a good place to start and then we can go from there."

Mrs. Goldstein put her elbows on the table and folded her hands. "Mrs. Donovan, I think you're a tad bit confused. You don't have a choice in this matter. Your husband has filed for divorce.

248

We also found out that he hired his divorce attorney a year and a half ago, so you see, he's been planning this for some time. Mrs. Donovan, I've been doing this for over thirty years and the fact that he took all of the money out of the bank accounts is not a good sign. That's why I asked Mr. Kellogg and his partner to join us today. They are the best forensic accountants money can buy. Mr. Kellogg is also a former FBI agent, so you see, you're in very good hands."

"I'm sorry. I don't understand," said Liv.

"May I call you Olivia?"

"Of course."

"Olivia, in my experience, men like your husband tend to hide their assets when they're going through a divorce."

"What do you mean?"

"How much money would you say your husband has been making the last five years?"

"If I had to guess, I'd say close to a million dollars a year."

"Well, I can assure you that he's not going to want to give you close to what you deserve as far as child support and alimony. Mr. Kellogg is going to make sure you get what you deserve. Now, did you bring all of your jewelry?"

"Yes," Liv said as she pulled her jewelry box out of a large tote bag.

"Helen," said Mrs. Goldstein, "can you please take pictures of all of the pieces and put them into our safe? Now, Olivia, did your husband give you all of these items?"

"Actually, no."

"Well the pieces he did not give you can go back home with you. And what about the jewelry you're wearing?"

Liv looked down at the ring Kurt had just given her. "He actually just gave me this for our anniversary two days ago."

"Unfortunately, that will have to go into the safe as well."

Liv slowly slid the ring off of her finger. Tears began running down her face. Mrs. Goldstein handed her a box of tissues. "I'm sorry," said Liv. "I just can't believe this is happening."

Liv's mom put her arm around her daughter. "I think she's just in shock," she said, turning toward Mrs. Goldstein. "And her health has not been the best these past few years." Then she explained all about Liv's medical condition.

"Well, excuse me for saying this," Mrs. Goldstein exclaimed, "but what a bastard! I've seen some horrible men over the years but I think your soon-to-be ex-husband takes the cake. But don't you worry. I promise you, you're in good hands. So before we end the meeting, I'm going to need you to sign the retainer page and I will also need a check."

Liv looked down at the signature page. The retainer was $25,000.

"I'm sorry, but I really can't sign this. Remember, he drained all of our bank accounts."

Liv's mom took out her checkbook. "I got this," she said, as she filled out the check. "Now, Mrs. Goldstein, make sure you protect my daughter and nail this asshole to the wall. I'm sorry, Liv, but what he has done to you and the children is unforgivable!"

The next two weeks were a whirlwind. Liv finally got a credit card and her mother took her to a local bank to open up accounts for herself and the children. The Gallagher family all decided to pitch in, giving Liv a loan of a little over $500,000 so she wouldn't have to worry, and the kids' lives could remain the same, at least for the time being.

After two weeks, there was still no word from Kurt. And as if Liv didn't already have enough on her plate, the charity's first golf event for POTS research was taking place in less than a month. The event planner had begged her to cancel, but Liv refused.

"I will not allow him to ruin this event," she declared. "There are too many people counting on me. I have over one hundred golfers signed up. Not to mention the fact that Dr. Grubb is flying in with his colleagues from the University of Toledo Medical Center. No, this event must, and will, go on as planned."

Now the only thing left to do was to find a new sponsor for the event. Kurt's company Eagle Armor had been the original sponsor, but no more. Luckily, David Santoro had stepped in to save the day with his company, the Ramshead Restaurant Group, as the new sponsor. He had come back into Liv's life and was once again right by her side.

As for Liv, she went quickly from being heartbroken to being incredibly pissed off. The only sadness she felt was when she looked at her beautiful children. She found herself wondering if she had what it would take to be both the mother and father to all four of them. She remembered something that her grandmother always told her: Family first. In the days to come, Olivia would cling to her grandmother's words like a life preserver, hoping that they would help her through the rough seas ahead. And at the end of the day, Olivia Whittaker knew that life must, and will, go on…

To be continued...

...in Samantha Dupree's forthcoming novel,
Promises Made...

Acknowledgments

This labor of love of mine would never have happened without the love and support of my family and friends. I would like to start by thanking my father, Peter, who is and will forever be my hero. And my mother, who as you know by now from reading this book, has been right by my side, showing me the true meaning of "family first."

I would also like to thank my four beautiful children. My sons were just boys when this story begins, but I'm happy to report that they have grown into three incredible men who have stood by their mother's side every step of the way. It's hard to believe that sweet baby Rose is almost a teenager. They say everything happens for a reason, and my daughter is definitely proof of that. She fills my home with joyful laughter and an endless supply of hugs on a daily basis.

Last, but certainly not least, I would like to thank all of my childhood friends at the Jersey Shore. Growing up together, our parents would open the screen door at 8:30 a.m. and say, "Just be home by dark." Our days were filled with bike rides, crabbing, body surfing, and, at dusk, manhunt. Later down the road, there was spin the bottle, a first kiss on the lifeguard stand, and lying under a blanket of stars as the bonfire roared. There would also be the taste of beer for the first time and dancing until the sun came up to the soundtrack of The Big Chill.

These are the relationships and friendships that I will always hold dear to my heart. They say we are "Jersey Strong." I would just say we appreciate and honor where and who we came from.

Hope to see you down at the shore sometime,

Samantha